Dedalus Europe 2012
General Editor: Mike]

Saturn

Jacek Dehnel

SATURN

BLACK PAINTINGS FROM THE LIVES OF THE MEN IN THE GOYA FAMILY

Translated by Antonia Lloyd-Jones

Dedalus

LOTTERY FUNDED

Published in the UK by Dedalus Limited,
24-26, St Judith's Lane, Sawtry, Cambs, PE28 5XE
email: info@dedalusbooks.com
www.dedalusbooks.com

ISBN printed book   978 1 907650 69 7
ISBN ebook   978 1 909232 34 1

Dedalus is distributed in the USA by SCB Distributors,
15608 South New Century Drive, Gardena, CA 90248
email: info@scbdistributors.com   web: www.scbdistributors.com

Dedalus is distributed in Australia by Peribo Pty Ltd.
58, Beaumont Road, Mount Kuring-gai, N.S.W. 2080
email: info@peribo.com.au

Publishing History
First published in Poland 2011
First published by Dedalus in 2012
First ebook edition in 2012

Saturn copyright © *Wydawnictwo W.A.B. 2011*
Translation copyright © Antonia Lloyd-Jones 2012

The right of Jacek Dehnel to be identified as the author & Antonia Lloyd-Jones as the
translator of this work has been asserted by them in accordance with the Copyright,
Designs and Patents Act, 1988.

Printed in Finland by Bookwell
Typeset by Marie Lane

A C.I.P. listing for this book is available on request.

The Author

Jacek Dehnel is a poet, novelist, painter and translator. He was born in 1980.

In 2005 he was one of the youngest ever winners of Poland's Kościelski Prize for promising new writers. He studied Polish literature at Warsaw University then wrote his PHD thesis on the Polish translations of Philip Larkin, some of whose poetry he has translated himself. He has published four volumes of his own poetry which has been widely translated including into English.

The Translator

Antonia Lloyd-Jones is a full-time translator of Polish literature.

Her published translations include fiction by several of Poland's leading contemporary novelists, including *The Last Supper* by Pawel Huelle, for which she won the Found in Translation Award 2008. Her most recent translations include *The Night Wanderers* by Wojciech Jagielski (Seven Stories, February 2012), reportage about the child victims of the Lord's Resistance Army and the events in Uganda which led to its emergence. She also translates biographies, poetry, and books for children.

For my mother, a painter

When the present provides little joy and the months ahead portend nothing but repetition, the way to cheat monotony is by storming the past. From what one cannot tell anyone about one's life, one extracts the tiny splinters and the little bits of fluff, and transfers them to the hearth of the Roman patricians or the domiciles of the ancient Hebrews.

Pascal Quignard, *Pascal Quignard le solitaire*

Tell me who invented the father, and show me the branch they hanged him on.

R.M.

I

Javier:

I came into the world on Disappointment Street. Only when I was eight or ten years old did I hear, while hiding in the pantry, our cook telling the knife grinder where that name came from: long ago four handsome *majos* were chasing a beautiful girl, running down our street, right here, just under the windows of our house, which wasn't yet standing, past the front of the shop selling perfumes and gold pendants which hadn't yet opened and where old don Feliciano wasn't working because he hadn't even been born; and this girl came running, oh how she ran, and those *majos* were chasing after her, oh how they chased her, until they caught her; and in their ardour they tore off whole pieces of her clothing, ripped off her mantilla and the shawl she held across her face – and then they stood rooted to the spot, for there beneath the silks and satins they saw putrid flesh, the skull of a corpse coated in dry skin, the yellow teeth grinning. As they scattered in all directions, in seconds the body had turned to dust, all the ribbons and flounces too, and from then on the place was known as Disappointment Street. So said the cook, holding her sides – as I saw through the keyhole in the pantry door – brawny, ruddy, illuminated by a stream of sparks, as the knife grinder, who didn't know the story because he came from somewhere outside Madrid, set a succession of knives and scissors to his spinning stone,

11

nodding and muttering between one rasp of metal and the next. But my father – even if he didn't actually say it, didn't actually spit it out with the other insults he hurled at me – always believed, I am utterly convinced of this, that the street was so named because I, Javier, was born in a house that stood on it, in a small upstairs chamber within the apartment of the portraitist and deputy director of the Santa Bárbara Royal Tapestry Factory, soon to be royal painter, Francisco Goya y Lucientes.

Francisco:

When Javier was born, still on Calle de Desengaño, the older children were no longer alive; neither the first born, Antonio, nor Eusebio, nor little Vicente, nor Francisco, nor Hermengilda; not even her name could help María de Pilar, the name by which we commended her to the care of Our Lady of Zaragoza. I never told Javier this – for in those days I tried not to pamper the children, but to bring up my son to be a real man, not like now, when my heart has gone soft and I have been turned into a teary old pantaloon, deaf as a post to boot, which is a great help in bearing the children's shrieks – and so: I never told Javier this, but when La Pepa gave birth to him and was lying in bed, exhausted, with strands of black hair stuck to her perspiring brow as the light falling from the window cast a great stain across it, as if of lead white, I rushed into the city and cried to all whom I knew and all whom I did not that there was no finer sight in Madrid than this boy.

After him we went on trying, fearing that he too would not stay with us for long; my dear departed wife, Josefa Bayeu, or simply La Pepa, if she were not dressing, was lying in bed – either in labour, or, if she had miscarried, with yet another haemorrhage. Once I even tried to count up, and it had happened twenty times. But, unfortunately, only Javier survived. Unfortunately only, and unfortunately Javier.

II

Old People

Old age is revolting. Its smells and textures. Runny eyes with bloodshot corners, balding eyelashes and brows, drooping folds of flesh, liver spots. Its gluttony as it sucks up the scraps, its greedy way of lunging for its bowl with loud slurping.

They say it is a fine thing for two people to grow old together. Does one become verminous and mangy in a finer way in company than on one's own? Of all the sabbats in the world the sabbat of old age is the most horrific, for which the young men come plodding instead of running, with masks made of wrinkled skin placed over their smooth faces.

The eye, no weaker than the rest of the body, sees only the strongest contrasts: a patch of light on the tip of the nose just above the dark line of the toothless mouth. Cadaverous, black shadows beneath overhanging brows, and around them the clear circles of the cheeks and forehead. The gleam of a silver spoon above the hollow of the plate, the slurping, the emaciated fingers emerging from the gloom of a wide sleeve. And the black pupils, enlarged by desire, surrounded by the whites of goggling eyes. Oh, to gorge oneself on life before it ends!

Oh, what disgust we feel when we look at our parents as they change into moulting, insatiable beasts, broken machinery, leaking vessels.

Oh, what incomprehension we feel as we look at our children when they see us as moulting, insatiable beasts, broken machinery, leaking vessels. Inside we are still a young lad with ambitions, who travels to the big city with just one small bundle; we are a young, not bad-looking girl, who says to herself: "Oh, life, we'll soon see who'll be the master of whom!"

III

Javier:

Life's good to him over there, in France. They tell me everything here. There he sits, a widower far from his wife's grave, satisfied, the old fox, the well-fed badger, the grizzled grouse, painting trite inanities, miniatures on ivory, doing nice little drawings; Leocadia makes him food, takes care of him and cuts his apples into quarters, in person, because he doesn't like the taste of the ones the servant prepares, and then she gives herself to anyone who happens along – there's no lack of opportunity in Bordeaux; apparently lately it's some German, who doesn't even know she isn't as *weiss* as she looks. Rosario, sorry, I mean *little Ladybird* – he never calls her anything but "little Ladybird" – sits beside him and they "create together". In a single flourish he draws something – not necessarily an image that is suitable for a little girl of her age, even if she is the daughter of a harlot and has seen a thing or two – and she crudely tries to repeat it. A curved line where it should be straight, a straight line where it should be curved, but above all a boring line. Boring, monotonous, charmless. Then the old man takes another sheet and – I can just see it, I can see it – muttering something incomprehensible to himself, just as he always has done, and if not always, then at least since he went deaf, in a single gesture turns a piece of paper into a banknote: a witch flying with a skipping rope, an old cuckold and his young

16

wifey (it never occurs to him that he's portraying himself), or a condemned man being garrotted; in short, a perfect drawing, for which I'd at once have several buyers. And he gives it to that little bantling. Blinking, fidgeting beside him on her chair, smiling now and then, she sticks out her little lizard tongue, surely inherited from her mother, and "shades it in", in other words she scrawls her dull strokes all over the folds of cloth, pieces of background, and clouds of hair, while the old man says "lighter", "darker", "lighter". And so, eagerly working away in league with each other, they change banknotes into scribbles good for nothing but rolling paper for tobacco.

Francisco:

Life's good to me over here in France, but it's bad to me here in old age. When the sunlight is strong – though not as strong as in Madrid – I can see better, and then I get down to some painting. I no longer have the strength for large canvases, in any case I can hardly move at all. There's a young fellow here who has escaped from Spain, de Brugada; he spends a lot of time with us and takes me for walks, and has even learned how to talk to me – not as before, when he wrote on scraps of paper that I found hard to decipher, but using his hands, according to Father Bonet's system. The day before yesterday I told him off for waving his paws about, as if he wanted to tell the whole neighbourhood that not only can old Goya hardly drag his pins along, but he's also deaf, deaf, deaf as a post, deaf as a stone, a brush, a doorknob, deaf as a bundle of old rags that moves by black magic. I must stink of piss, for I have an ailing bladder, but I can't smell it myself, I haven't my old sense of smell that could sniff out a juicy quim coming down the street... I can just see how others grimace when I come too near, but as they don't want to cause me grief they hide their scowls, which is even more humiliating. I wear three pairs of spectacles. Three pairs of spectacles on one big snout. Not the biggest one at that. My sight is failing me, and so are my hands. I am lacking in everything, except willpower.

For some time I worked on lithographs, I drew bulls from memory... Brugada helped me, he set the stone on the easel, he fixed it in place, and then I scrawled away at it, scratched away with a razor, holding a large magnifying glass in my other hand, for without it I could hardly see a thing – but twice the stone broke free of the easel, once it came close to crushing my foot, just scraping the edge of my boot, and the second time it thudded to the floor with little Rosario standing only three paces away. Of course all my work was for nothing. And that second time I had a beautiful scene, almost finished. I gave up on it. I have even less strength for large canvases, but my little Ladybird has grown big enough to paint by now, and I'm thinking of sending her to Paris to study, I've even dispatched a couple of letters, perhaps Ferrer would find her a place at Martin's – apparently he's not bad. It won't be a waste of money, because there is someone to train, not like that arse Javier, who is incapable of getting down to anything, but just lies about like a larva, like a fatty lump of meat in a roasting tin, in its congealed juices; he doesn't fancy coming to see me, he doesn't fancy hauling that obese rear-end of his across the Pyrenees, so I, an old boy, must travel there and back again like a young lark, or else I'll never see my lovely Marianito. As if they couldn't drop their business for a while – anyway, what sort of business do they have there? – to come and see their father who has one foot in the grave. But there is little Ladybird, it's worth spending time on Ladybird, I even showed her drawings in Madrid – all the professors at the Academy were thrilled and said she was like a little Raphael in skirts, like a little Mengs in satins. Compared with her, Mengs is a pipsqueak. The world has never seen such a talent before. So we sit together, I draw something for her on a scrap of paper, and she carefully copies it – how much industry there is in it, how much fluency, what a lovely line! There's no expertise yet, it's true, but you can sense genius. Goya can sense genius. So she does her drawing, Leocadia bustles about the house or goes out to the town; after all, a woman has to get something out of life, we are in France, not in Spain, I'm not going to keep her at home under lock and key, am I? So she draws, I fetch some small flakes of ivory out of the drawer, some paints and very thin brushes, then looking through my magnifying glass, first I lay a dark undercoat of soot taken from the lamp, then I drip a few drops of water onto it. What worlds are there, how many figures are teeming there, how many ghosts and desires – cripples, prisoners, pot-bellied dwarves, old witches; I look through my glass and am filled with amazement at how much can be happening on such a tiny tile, as the water dissolves the soot. And then, chop-chop, I set about painting. If it doesn't come out well, and more and more often it doesn't, I scrape it off without regret, because I know that water dissolves black in full harmony with the current of my thoughts, and will immediately summon up something even better. Something more painful.

I used to sit with Javier too, just as I do with little Ladybird – I used to think to myself that if my dear papa, a common gilder, had spawned an artist like me, then what would my son achieve! So I thought about all of them in turn: about Antonio, Eusebio, Vicente and Francisco, but they all died, few of them lived long enough to be able to hold a pencil in his hand, let alone to amaze the world with his talent; even with Javier so many times it was just a step, just a whisker away – like the time when he had smallpox and I carried him in my arms all night long, instead of doing some painting or humping some wench; burning with fever, exhausted from crying, he would fall asleep for a moment, then at once wake up again; when I told the king about it he was so moved that he seized me by the hand and shook it for a long time, and then began to play the violin, which was probably meant to bear witness that the old dotard felt for me. And since he did not have a second fiddler behind the curtain to play the difficult passages, as he did during performances before the court, and since I was not yet deaf, I did not find it easy... Oh well, each man sympathizes by whatever practice he can afford – by means of my masterpieces I showed sympathy for all of living, bleeding Spain, he showed sympathy for a sick child and his father by sawing away at the fiddle. And a good thing too. But not just that time, either; all through Javier's childhood I did my best not to get accustomed to him; I was afraid he would depart this life like the son before, or like the ones Pepa miscarried afterwards: bloody shreds, filth on the sheets, monstrosities that I would prefer, like so many other horrors, not to have before my eyes, but I can see them all the time – when I close my eyes, when I'm sleeping, or waking, as I gaze at a drop of water dissolving the black on a tile of ivory, I see not just corpses shot dead against a wall, not just nuns raped by French mercenaries, but those hideous things that came out of her too: dwarves, homunculi that would fit on the palm of your hand; one with an overgrown head, another with no legs at all, horrible, horrible.

But one survived, and it was with him that I used to sit

as I now do with Rosario – ah, those were the finest times, when I could see how he was becoming a faithful copy of his own father, bah, his, that is *my* masterwork; how he took the brushes from their case, the spatulas, pieces of wire and corapora, how he examined various pigments and asked what they were made of... and yet there was no genius in him; I could sense that almost from the very start, but I deceived myself that something would still grow out of him; what an idea. For chattering, prattling on about pigments, about colours he was the first – but when he had to set about the canvas, or the paper, he was so fussy, so timid, now he was too shy, now he couldn't do it, now this, now that; until sometimes I thought he was doing it on purpose, to spite me, so I told him off a few times, gave him a good hiding as you do a boy, and after that it got even worse. He didn't want to paint with me, he didn't want to come to the studio, he was more and more indolent and taciturn. I don't know where he got it from, certainly not from me. It appears to come from his mother. But though indeed taciturn, she was a hard-working woman. She didn't know much, nor did she say much, all the better. She just liked to get dressed up. But don't all women like to do that?

Javier:

Not that he didn't allow me to sit beside him like that too. He did. As long as he was in Madrid, of course, as long as he was in a good mood and had at least a tiny bit of consideration for me; for sometimes he would paint for days on end, furiously, muttering compound insults under his breath, and then he would continue long into the night, in a top hat to which he would attach several candles, always of the best quality, which gave the strongest and whitest light possible; if there were none of those left, he made a scene, woke my mother and the servants, and sent somebody to the shop to bang on the door until the owner got up, opened it and sold the best-quality candles for Señor de Goya, the well-known raving lunatic. And he would also go on trips – he would get a commission here or there, paint a minister at his estate or a countess at her palace, or a large canvas for some church, which he must of course see with his own eyes to know where the light fell from, the exact shade of the stone the walls were made of when it changed colour in the sunlight, from what distance and from what angle it would be looked at, and thus what foreshortening to apply. He would vanish for whole weeks at a time, no matter whether for his work or to go hunting with his school-friend, Zapater... He merely informed my mother; anyway, even if she had known what he sometimes said about himself and about Alba, even if he had told her: I'm going to see the duchess and I intend to have a very good time, she would only have lowered her gaze, because that was all she was capable of doing. Well, and laying herself wide open to him, if the time came for yet another pregnancy, yet another miscarriage.

But when I was nine years old, he went away for ages – not that it didn't happen often, but this time he disappeared for longer than he had predicted; letters came from Cadiz, but written in someone else's hand – by then I could already recognize his sloping, rather crooked handwriting with long whiskery *s*'s and *y*'s – my mother would sit in her room for days on end, or in a sudden fit would come running in to me and start to hug and kiss me, urgently, excessively, so that I wanted to break loose of those starched cuffs and stiff lace as fast as possible; if in my struggle I happened to glance at her, I would see that her eyes were all puffy from weeping, with thin red rings around them, so bloodshot that the whites were entirely pink; her features would have coarsened with despair, just as they often did when she was pregnant; she looked pitiful, so I only had to peep at her, and I hadn't the heart to go on trying to escape, but would freeze like a sparrow caught in a net when taken hold of, and I would wait for her to satisfy her need for an insistent embrace. But generally I managed to avoid the sight of her face, I wriggled to right and left like a wild thing, rather than have to look at her – then I could break free and run away to the kitchen or the patio.

He came back horribly wasted away – the coachman and the servant actually carried him into the house, leaning on their arms – he was bluish, greenish, as if moulded from dirty wax, horribly emaciated, with his head wrapped in a white scarf; but the strangest thing was the almost total silence that accompanied this scene. No joyful shouts, no greetings, no issuing of orders; if my mother had to say anything, she said it in a whisper, as if afraid to disturb the solemn silence. Every rustle of her dress, every tap of her heel seemed too loud.

Only that evening, as the serving maid put me to bed, did she tell me: "You poor child, now your papa is totally deaf".

After that he lay in bed for a few months more – his face filled out, he started drawing in a notebook, and being grumpy, like the typical recovering patient. He was constantly calling for something or losing his temper because he couldn't paint; and as he had gone deaf he was terribly noisy; his powerful voice could be heard all over the house, from don Feliciano's shop on the ground floor, where it made the glass vials of perfume gently shake and jingle, right up to the attic, where it set the drying sheets asway. "Javieeer," he screamed, "Javieeer, come to your papaaa!" and I would run off wherever I could, just as earlier I had run from my mother's possessive clasp.

Having a handicap means being a stranger. A man who

has lost a hand is by no means the same man as before, but simply without a hand. He is a man who instead of a hand has a hand missing, a completely new body part which one may not look at, and which one should not mention, to avoid causing distress. For just as instead of a hand, the body now has a hand missing, so the soul too, instead of something, has something missing, a painful, festering, sensitive organ. And those who lose a sense, lose incomparably more – the whole world accessible only by means of that sense; bah, even more than that. Not just the tune of the *zarzuelas*, not just the way in which La Tirana uttered the words from the stage, with that burbling chirruping in your ear, that cooing, but the murmur of whispers drifting across the auditorium, the cries coming from the furthest rows, the bravos, that communal wave of noises by which everyone, in unison, thanked her for the sounds that she had delivered from behind the footlights, like two seas opposite each other – the spectators' hundreds of throats against her one, unparalleled throat. And the *sainetes* that used to make him roar with laughter, all those little scenes with crafty orange girls and gallant *majos*, with opinionated doctors and smart street urchins who always get their way – oh, he used to learn the songs by heart and sing them afterwards while working, even years on, when he couldn't hear himself and was horribly out of tune; all this he lost. Nor was there any more dressing himself up to go out, squeezing himself into the braided jackets and gold-edged breeches he was so proud of (though it was a long time since he had had the waist of a *torero*, which my mother never failed to mention under her breath)... And the scores he used to send to his beloved Zapater, the scores of the *sainetes* and *seguidillas*, how much trouble he would have with that, running about the stalls to get the latest hits! He would pack them all up and send them by post-horse to Zaragoza, and when he came home he'd say: "That is my last farewell to music – let Martín enjoy it, from now on I'm never going back to the places where I could hear those songs... I've told myself I must stick to some damned principles, and maintain a certain damned dignity that's due to a man!" – and thus he would mutter to himself the whole way back to the house, but even so that night he would go out, dressed in one of his embroidered *majo* jackets, and laugh himself to tears at others who were just like him. But the moment he lost his hearing, he never put on a *majo* jacket again, not even for a joke, as if those were the clothes of a dead man.

Francisco:

There are things it is impossible to talk about. You can only paint them. And to tell the truth, not even that is possible either.

Javier:

And so he dragged himself from bed to the easel a stranger. Above all a stranger to us, for no words were getting through to him; he would sit in his studio like a fish in a dark, brown tank covered in unusual algae – rolls of canvas, the skeletons of picture stretchers, and scraped-off paint – and work without respite, often at night, which meant he used even more candles than before, and his clothes and the entire studio floor were spattered in pearly trails and drops of wax; he took every single commission, anything to prove he could still paint, and started going to meetings at the Academy, to put a stop to all the rumours that "Goya is finished", which the malicious daubers were spreading, and he'd sit at those gatherings, not understanding a word, but making – or so I imagine – a wise face, as if he could hear every last little word and was weighing it profoundly; he painted terrifying pictures on tin – a fire, shipwrecks on a bare rock, bandits butchering travellers, a prison, madmen teeming in hospital corridors; to this day I have entire scenes stamped upon my memory: faces twisted in terror, distorted hands, despairing gestures; I would creep up as close as possible and watch from a hiding place, from behind a canvas or a chair, as panting, muttering, moving away from the picture and running back up to it, he applied the greasy, oily black of manacles to the canvas, splashes of white foam spraying a corpse, red-and-brown, dry stains – blood soaking into the sand under the wheels of a stagecoach. If he realized I was standing nearby – noticing me out of the corner of his eye, on feeling my breath tickling the back of his left hand when he let it drop, or simply on sensing someone's presence, somebody's attention focused on him, as happens to any of us at times, he would turn round abruptly and drive me out of the door; sometimes this bore the hallmarks of a game: he would hoot, bark and growl menacingly, and tickle me under the arms; but as a rule he was truly angry, especially when he was painting a scene from the madhouse – at once he covered it with a sheet and seized hold of a wooden slat or a rag to chase me out of the studio. Then he sent the picture off with a letter to Zapater – I don't know what his heirs have done with it – and painted himself another one, exactly the same, a few years later. In any case, I was unable to communicate with him. He could not yet lip-read, and I was almost unable to write; he would lose patience as I slowly and laboriously set down each letter in turn, and he would try to guess the words; if he succeeded, he would wait for the next one, then try to guess the one after that, but at some point he would forget what the first word had been, and grow even more furious. That was when I realized why we had a large house. Large houses are for escaping. And if someone is deaf it is even easier to hide from him; you can run from room to room right behind his back – but lightly, so that his feet won't feel the floor shuddering; when you are ten years old you can run lightly, as light as a feather. I learned to write quickly and clearly, so that our conversations should last as short a time as possible, and this seemed to bring on the desire to read – my father was not fond of books, my mother only had a missal, but at my school, run by the priests, apart from some dreadfully boring screeds of prayers, there were a few interesting books from better times, long ago. Once I had grown up a bit and had more audacity, I used to ask some of my father's acquaintances to tell me which books they especially valued, and if I couldn't find them in the Piarists' library, on their next visit I would beg to borrow them; of course I wasn't allowed to pester the guests in the drawing room, but I could stand before them (straight as a ramrod, with sweaty hands) in the hall as they entered or exited the house; I often got a clip round the ear from the serving maid or from my parents, but sometimes the desired book was later put into my hands, and I would rush straight off to my room to start reading it. Señor Martínez, who one time came for a longer stay on business from Cadiz and was quite often at our house, tried to persuade my father to send me to school abroad, but he replied curtly: "Javier is a painter. A born painter. He gets it from me. Any studying except for the study of painting is a waste of time for him. Not to mention money. And the same goes for books. A damned waste. He squanders so much good light."

But above all, on going deaf my father became a stranger to himself, to his former self; he changed his habits, his tone of voice, and his way of working; he lost his temper over anything at all. It is true he always was a hothead, but now he was like a wolf caught in a trap, which bites anyone who happens to come along, even though every jump and snap of its teeth make the snares dig deeper into the flesh and bone of its paw.

IV

Woman with a Knife

The sharp arches of the raised eyebrows, ringed with blue-green shadows, testify to sympathy – and who knows, maybe Malady does sympathize with the sick man whom she is consuming; but she has not come here out of sentiment; she has work to do; she has gathered her hair on the top of her head and tied it in a scarf, rolled her sleeves up high like a diligent maid who is about to clean a room and rid it of unwanted clutter. But why has she exposed her breasts, which with their tips barely covered by the thick folds of a crumpled shirt, are glowing with the grey gleam of a sick body? Out of pity, so there would be something to look at in the moment of greatest menace, just before the slashing, as the knife fell with a swish and cut off what it had to cut off, for once and for all?

How easily something is taken away. Everywhere, all around, someone is refusing somebody something, disinheriting, depriving somebody of something; in the crowd it's a watch, cut off with a nimble action; at the tribunal, it is freedom; in bed, in tangled sheets, it's virginity; such is the order of the world. Thus Malady does not particularly have to sympathize, she just diligently does her work, which is part of a large, indispensable whole – from constant chopping she has solid muscles; the knife has been sharpened so many times that its end is too short, snapped off perhaps against a stubborn limb, or a sense that held onto the flesh tightly.

The victim is quite another matter – it is extremely hard to be bereft. Look how desperately he seizes her arm – only the thumb is visible, slipping down the rolled-up sleeve, and a flesh-coloured triangle – a scrap of the arm, with which he shields his head, sensing where the blow will fall. Every sinew of the body, every muscle is trying to get it out of the trap; almost all of him has rolled out of the picture; his face is invisible, and a good thing too, for if I had to paint him, my hand would shake with emotion. Of course he can sense the slash to come – the instant pain, the stickiness of blood spurting from the wound, weakness in the knees, deep black lakes flooding the eyes. But he cannot yet sense the identical twin stroke that deprives him of whole vast expanses of life, which seem to him obvious; afterwards he will see them somewhere inside, in a dream perhaps, in the form of a succession of rooms, beautifully furnished, full of the people dearest to him. The doors of these rooms violently slam shut, set moving by an inexplicable force, until he is left entirely alone in a long corridor, with those dark doors stretching in rows down either side of it, slammed shut forever and ever amen.

But for now he is suspended in this brief moment, when the knife is still hanging, before it falls; in the corner of his eye he can see that a third, dark figure, whose hand is raised in a gesture – so he thought – of sympathy, is just a silent wooden statue; and the sympathetic face of Malady is a mask made of whitewashed cardboard, behind which nobody knows who is hiding.

V

Javier:

Only when I was grown up and married myself, just before Mariano's birth, did I suddenly realize, in fact while thinking about something completely different, that the picture of Our Lady of Zaragoza in my parents' bedroom had a frame with a special curtain that could be drawn at any moment, purely because it hung above the matrimonial bed, where my father so often fulfilled his nuptial duties to my mother, and my mother fulfilled hers to my father. And that the large cloth, which always hung on a peg in the corner of the studio served for exactly the same purpose: for shielding a holy picture during the siesta, when my father would lock the door and "think about painting", for which he required "complete solitude" although he never turned the model out of the room. Or models, if there were more of them just then.

Only once I had grown up myself and was painting, or rather, when I was often thinking about painting, did I realize that he didn't need the models at all; in any case not as other artists do, who would arrange some wenches hired for a few *maravedís* in the poses of nymphs and goddesses – leaning against a wall, lying on boxes, wrapped in an old rag pretending to be gorgeous silks – and draw the lines of the shadows precisely: they would look where the light separated from the darkness, where the border was fluid, and where sharp; how the perspective changed a knee, a hand, or an inclining nape into

32

incomprehensible shapes. He knew the body by heart: female, male, animal. Alive or dead. Unconscious. Skewered on a tree stump or slit wide open. A horse's withers, the muscles of a bull's neck playing under the thick hide, the gnarled fingers of poor folk, the quivering fat on the belly of a fishwife being carried by witches to their sabbath. He knew the lights and shades typical of each body, the plexuses and perspectives; all that theatre, positioning arms and legs, casting on drapery and turning towards the sunlight was entirely superfluous to him – and yet the girls came to pose, even when he was painting pictures without a single woman in them. He did hasty sketches of them – he left whole wads of these drawings in Madrid, which I later pasted into albums – as they were letting down their hair, sitting on a stool holding a folded fan, straddling a travelling chest, or gazing at their own image in a small mirror, held overhead in both hands. The fact that he had them, first of all on paper, and then – either after or in the course of the work – on the chest, against the wall, leaning on the easel, variously, became a part of the painting, even if it depicted executed insurgents, Wellington on his horse or a bullfight; it was they, the orange sellers from Manzanares, the washerwomen, the serving girls, who entered the warp and weft of the canvas, the tackiness of the primer, the paints, and the powdered pigments. Just the same as the slaughtered grouse, hares or deer that he brought down as soon as he took aim to shoot. He could not create something out of nothing – first he had to lay his hands on something, to have some other, live thing emerge from under them later.

My mother either pretended not to see this, or really didn't see it – maybe she complained about it to her confessor, maybe to the Virgin Mary Herself, or maybe, as the younger sister of an artist, she thought it must simply be like that, because

33

naked women in the house are just as much a fact of life for an artist's wife as wiping away the white dust that settles on all the furniture, or putting up with the smell of paints and turpentine, not to mention putting up with scenes and rows? I don't know.

When my father left his parental home, his mother gave him her blessing and a small notebook, in which – having consulted a well connected uncle – she had written out for him the names of the most important people in all of Spain: dukes, judges, bishops and ministers. Once he had painted Count Floridablanca, his first major portrait, in which he himself stands in the shadow, tiny, timidly presenting the picture to the slender minister, squeezed into a red frock coat – in reality a runt of a man two heads smaller than he – he could put the first tick against a name in the notebook. Evidently, he would remain forever the humble servant in this large, ugly painting; he thought it a small price to pay for the commissions that followed, which really did start to pour in, one after another. Year upon year he crossed out some names and wrote in others, ticking off successive rulers, ambassadors, duchesses and generals. He did it in the reigns of King Charles and King Ferdinand, under the French and the British, without any difference.

Can this man, at the age of twenty-seven and with nothing but tireless ambition to his name, on looking at a not particularly pretty girl (forgive me, Mama!), have failed to consider the fact that her brother, his fellow pupil at Luzán's school, Francisco Bayeu, Mengs's favourite, belonged to the Royal Academy of San Fernando and had the post of royal painter? When he called himself a pupil of Bayeu, and not Luzán, did he know that would earn him interest in its time? Just like putting his tail between his legs when Rámon Bayeu

voted for his own brother in the Academy's annual contest?
First the wedding, then the commissions, the position at the
Royal Tapestry Factory, the move to Madrid... but someone
will always remind an arriviste that he came out of the dry,
cracked earth in Fuendetodos – and when he quarrelled with
his brother-in-law Francisco while painting the cupolas in
Zaragoza cathedral, and when with his friend, the lawyer
Zapater, he ground out a long appeal to the cathedral canons,
and when at last he was recommended Christian humility and
gave in, although he eventually painted what his brother-in-
law told him to, and as he told him to, even so in the end he
was shown his place. Three medals were minted to mark the
painting of the cupola: one each for Francisco, Rámon and
Josefa Bayeu. Yes, for my mother, who never once held a
brush in her hand, apart perhaps from the rare moments when
she managed to tidy the studio. Her husband, the little man
from nowhere, had to be satisfied with his fee, like a common
workman.

I'd swear he paid her back for that in some way.

To be an unloved woman all your life – that is even harder
than to be an unloved man all your life.

Francisco:

I have much to thank God for in life – certainly not for
bestowing genius and money on me, because both my genius
and my money I earned for myself through hard toil, but for
giving me a loving heart, open to manifold affection. I loved
my dear wife, I loved each of my children, including Javier,
I loved my Marianito, and in my way, even my daughter-in-
law; when La Pepa died, my heart opened to Leocadia, a poor
lost soul, unhappy with a mean, dry husband – can anyone be

35

happy with a jeweller, a man who converts everything into carats? – and then to Ladybird, little Rosario. Yes, my heart was open to all varieties and versions of love, even of the kind I would prefer to forget and would be afraid to mention; for the whole time, out of divine grace, like a bloodhound tracking a wounded deer, it was constantly on the move. As long as it beats, it gives chase.

To some men God gives noble birth, to others beauty, yet others a prick like a mule, and to me He gave this insatiable hunger which has driven me all my life. How different we are from one another when indulging our more unruly parts! If there are medical men capable of drivelling on for hours at a time about nothing but what they can see in a small vial of piss, then if I were a writer, rather than a painter, I would write a learned treatise hundreds of pages long on what can be said about a woman merely by looking at her hole, and how that hole behaves. Well, several holes, let us say. At the very thought of it my investigative organ becomes strangely sprightly, despite the eighty years that both of us, my organ and I, have lately come to bear.

In all my life I have only known one single human being who understood the richness of knowledge emanating from what others regard as plain old humping. La Alba! That was no woman – that was a man with a slender waist, long black hair, and fine paps, that was the most powerful person in the kingdom. They said of her that she could have crossed the whole of Spain from one end to the other without ever leaving her own land; that is the truth. But they were only talking about property – yet if she had insisted, she really would have walked across the whole of Spain, through the worst wildernesses, through forest lairs full of brigands, in nothing but a pair of ballroom slippers!

Even children stopped playing their games to look at her.

How painstakingly she would write out long stories in my notebook, as if she wanted to tell me her entire life, and how I regretted that I could not hear her voice! Sometimes I used to imagine it: low and melodious, husky when she was angry, and gentle at times of tenderness. And despite being so strong, she had so much tenderness in her that she could have bestowed it on a dozen women and a dozen men, for she had in her both female and male, twofold tenderness.

She used to have whores brought for me from Cadiz, sweet little strumpets, and she would write me a note to say that she had told the coachman, to whom she would entrust this delicate matter, to choose the ones that looked the most like her; that made him blush terribly, the stupid dolt. But he would go and fetch them from the port taverns, brawny, tanned, with a shock of black curls. And I would draw them. Sometimes La Alba was present the while – she would sit in a comfortable armchair carried in specially from the terrace, and she would play with a monkey or with the Little Negress, María de la Luz, the small daughter of her black slavegirl, and I would tell the whores to assume ever-changing poses. "Now," I would say, "I am to paint a saint for an altar near Zaragoza, this one would be perfect! Let the pious venerate the immoral!" She would watch over my shoulder and start to laugh – I could feel her breath on my ear – as my hand moved especially quickly, and swish swoosh, a little figure appeared on the page: ruffling her black hair, removing a chamber pot, or sweeping the floor. "I could spend my whole life sweeping the floor," she wrote down for me, "it's more interesting than being me." But she herself would never have posed for me with a broom. Or with a chamber pot. Sometimes she insisted that I sleep with one of the girls. "Goya, give yourself some relief," she wrote. I refused. She probably regarded that as rather ungrateful, and would pout. In the end she used to send them to her poor little monk, Brother Basilio – he was never fussy and always took advantage. He was a proper scrounger: such an oaf, such a hare-brained fool, who would stammer and fall off the mule the duchess had presented him with, that he might ride everywhere in her retinue, but he knew how to set about his own affairs. One time he went sprawling from that mule into a ditch, and smeared himself with mud, a most pitiful sight; the entire entourage stopped, and everyone guffawed at the little monk as he clambered onto the road, slipped back down, then clambered up again; by now the duchess was jumping off her horse, now she was flying, in her white dress, now she was offering him her hand, showering him in kisses, and covering herself in dirt, wearing all those mud stains on her white dress and her red sash like medals; she turned to them all and said: "He alone understands me, from the very start I have always known that he alone has a soul just like mine". And so he put on some fat, and lived it up, the little horror – good luck to him, I do not grudge him anything. It wasn't me he exploited, it wasn't at my expense that he ate all those sweetmeats. And what about Lusito? He was a lovely little thing, a dream of a boy, curly-haired and charming, with fire in his eyes – she called him her darling little son, he carried scents and sorbets after her. Or La Beata, a beast incarnate, her old duenna, who saw devils everywhere; she was shrunken, with a white face, as if dusted with rice powder, a walking arthritic corpse, tripping along beneath her dress as if she were a slow, wind-up toy. I used to draw caricatures of her – Alba adored that. I even painted two of them; in one the Little Negress and Lusito are tugging at the hem of La Beata's dress, and she is baring her teeth at them like a furious capuchin monkey, in the other she is warding off Alba with a crucifix as she tries to put rouge on the old woman's lips. "Come here," she laughed, "we'll paint your little skeleton so the other corpselets will like it, when the time comes!"

And as for me, what about me? I was one of her fixtures, I was a courtier, I was her beloved Deaf-Adder, just as Lusito was her Little Sonny-boy, La Beata was Morta, don Basilio was the Stutterer, and María de la Luz was her Little Negress. We were her collection of outcasts, rejects and cripples. She had a tortoise with one leg missing and a monkey with no tail. "My grandfather, who brought me up," she once wrote down for me, "the twelfth duke of Alba, had a lopsided dwarf, Benito, who always walked ahead of him, with all his master's medals pinned to his puny, crooked chest. That taught me to despise riches and honours for good and all." And how clearly she made her point, how energetically! A clearly made point like that is a work of art in itself. It is no surprise that she bequeathed us her entire fortune, a quarter of Spain. Well, maybe not a quarter. And maybe not her entire fortune, but a large part of it. She was the last Duchess of Alba – her husband took her surname so that the clan would not die out, but he died, without giving her a child. Not very industrious, I would say. It all went to some people called Stuart, none of her menagerie of oddities got a penny except for me – but I did not request it for myself. I asked for Javier, who in those days was still the loveliest sight in Madrid.

Javier:

The older he was, the more he liked to talk about his past conquests. He would spout obscenities, until white froth appeared in the corners of his mouth. And in such detail!

After all those years he couldn't remember as many as half his paintings, but he could recite the name of every girl he had encountered here or there, retell with precision the most tasteless anecdotes concerning just about every single body with which he had ever had, as I might put it, close contact. And yet – he never said straight out that the duchess had let him come closer to her than her ancestry would allow, or as permitted by the innumerable ducal, marquesal, comital and baronial titles that poured down on her from all branches of her family tree like the tributaries of a river merging into a single stream. Or, to put it in his language, he never said whether she had had it off with him.

I know that in the palace Alba hung up her official portrait in a white dress, with red bows and sash – it is sure to be still hanging there – but few people know that a second portrait has been hanging in my father's house for all these years, corresponding to that one in form and cast. But black. Her long, straight finger points at the sand, on which something has been written, and then smoothly painted over. If you look at it under the light, here and there you can see the shapes of letters hidden under the top coat of paint: *solo Goya*.

He was deaf and lonely. Lonely, because he was deaf. Whereas she loved anything that was rejected, imperfect, ailing: lunatics and failures, the ugly and the crippled. How could she have failed to take in a deaf painter for her collection of living curiosities? And as he ticked off surname after surname of the magnates of Spain in the notebook given him by his mother, how could he have failed to fall in love with the duchess, all of whose titles were hard to fit on a single sheet of paper?

Jacek Dehnel

Francisco:

I am eighty years old, and with every year less and less connects me with my life, because I remember less and less of it – I think that when I die, all I will have left is a single thin little thread which will be easy to break with the slightest movement. There are so many things I cannot remember! My parents' faces. My children's faces – to tell the truth, I can hardly even remember Javier's face, and when I want to bring him to mind, I look at a drawing I scrawled just before leaving Madrid. But that is the face of an adult, with sagging jowls. Not the sweet little face that used to hide in the folds of Pepa's skirts.

And of course, shame to admit, there are some women whom I don't remember either. I do not even know if I ever had Alba – anyway, what would that mean: to have her? Like other women? Do not make me laugh. It would be like having a wave, or catching a cloud in your net, or grasping a flame.

I had far more with her than rolling about in sweaty sheets, moaning and panting, far more than the sticky touch of foul-smelling crannies of the body: the common conviction that if a person were just a person, and not a list of titles, the owner of goods, a collection of bonds and responsibilities towards God and the kingdom, no one would have been happier than we. Each morning and each evening I would have said "*solo Alba*" and she would have said "*solo Goya*", a small farmstead would have been enough for our entire world, where we would have lived, I in a *majo* jacket and breeches, she dressed like a *maja*, a couple of happy peasants, surrounded by the freaks that I would have kept endlessly painting, while she would endlessly kiss and tug me by the ears.

But we both knew that was nonsense. When I painted her in mourning, I said: "It is not for your husband, it is for me." She looked at me as if she were about to burst into tears or fly into a fury, then she bit her lower lip and wrote: "Life is too short. Paint me in white."

Javier:

He came from Cadiz with just one painting, the lady in black. "The duchess didn't like it," he said, standing on the table in his studio and driving a large hook into the wall, "but I like it very much. It will hang here." And straight afterwards he told the serving girl to bring a piece of cloth large enough for him to be able to cover it from time to time. "Whenever I want to concentrate."

VI

Shamelessness

The boy who is walking past only sees them for a moment – he turns around, and from the dense blackness the light picks out his youthful, almost childlike profile. He casts a glance. If he had been looking consciously, he would have known what to expect, and he would have turned his eyes away quicker, but as it is, unintentionally, he remains in his turn a fraction too long and sees everything.

The younger woman still has all her teeth, and her laughter can be called laughter; the one who hasn't even black stumps left, eaten away by disease or knocked out with a chair leg by a drunken lover, the one with the puffy face and the matted hair, can only cackle now.

The forearm peeping out from under a sleeve rolled up as if for work, and moving steadily, is dark brown: tanned by the sun, and just plain dirty. With the dirt that covers everything around here: the unwashed hair, the ragged skirt made of thickly woven cloth, the shirt stained with brown-and-grey streaks on the neck edge.

From where we are standing the essence of the matter is not visible – but the toothless, wide-open jaws with the raspberry-pink bead of the tongue glinting in the corner is telling enough for us to understand just as much as the passing boy, who before turning his gaze away, stares for a fraction too long at the hand thrust under the skirt. It is from there that shivers emanate in all directions, it is from there that titillation radiates, it is that hand, its repeated motions, that are stretching the younger woman's lips into a smile, as she quivers right behind the other one's back (she is sitting so close that she can feel her shuddering in the thigh that is touching her mighty rump).

The boy who is walking past sees the very bottom of the blackness, the point of origin, hiding in the thick folds. He does not yet know that he himself came from right here, that the entire rest of the world came from here – the door into which he is going seems to him a salvation; he turns his gaze away, and quickens his pace. Twofold laughter chases after him, sniggering and cackling, blended with twofold fitful breathing.

VII

Javier:

Yes, of course I drew. I even painted. Despite my father's evasion, his shouting, his outbursts of monstrous anger when something didn't come out right in a picture – the colour was badly laid, the previous layer of glaze was coming off, the hand appeared too long, though up to that point it had looked quite correct – I felt drawn to his studio, and to painting itself. I didn't like the whole technical side: grinding the pigments, mixing them with binder, looking to see if the consistency was too thin or too thick, washing the brushes – I always reckoned painting should be a fine, pure art, not something between the crude work of a plasterer, boring pharmaceutical precision and the mundane labour of a chambermaid. It seemed to me that my old man, with all his splattering, hawking, spitting on the floor, his way of wiping the dirty brushes on anything that stood or lay within reach, tossing dirty rags on the floor and picking them up again if he had to wipe off excess impasto and didn't feel like looking for a new cloth – in short, for all that struck the eye upon entering the studio, he was a sort of swindler, impersonating a real painter, who should be painting calmly, with a relaxed forehead, in a fine, rich costume, like the ladies and gentlemen he portrayed; the lines should have been smooth and harmonious, the colours pleasant to the eye, the themes pleasant to the heart.

As time passed, the more I grew out of my fondness for Mengs's slick pictures and learned to value what the old man was doing – the roughness of the contours, the wild zigzags of light on embroidery, the violent contrasts – the more I regarded, and continue to regard his method of painting as repulsive to this day; not long ago I still used to wake up from a nightmare in which my father takes my freshly finished painting in his filthy, dirty paws and leaves huge, greasy brown stains on it, which nothing could possibly remove. "It's nothing, it's nothing," he always said in that dream, "it's even better like that, a bit of shadow down the sides."

I inherited my father's habit of carrying a sketchpad about with me; my one was always very smart and nicely kept, bound in dark morocco leather with embossed gold along the edges. There I jotted down the shapes of dogs, cats, wandering tradesmen, wild patterns drawn on the walls of houses in sharp sunlight by the shadows of street lamps and carved balustrades; I reproduced the line of a horse's back, the white sheen on his well-brushed rump, the coarse coat of a mule, the joint effort of branches bending in an autumn wind; the shape of my mother's nose and brow as she sat hunched over her embroidery, or the cook's serious, attentive face, if she found a moment to pose for me. I didn't write a diary, because I didn't think a young boy like me had much of interest to say about the world – but he can reproduce, jot down, record its wonderful, enchanting wealth, from the smallest drops of water on a plate to great chains of mountains. That seemed to me a good thing in itself alone.

I did my best not to show these drawings to my father – for him anything that was not full of witches, violence and filth was uninteresting; but whenever he saw that I was drawing, he came up, scowled and said something like: "Hey, you little dumpling, you're not catching the likeness – just look," and he'd cover the drawing in thick, dark lines. "See, here's the nose, yes, this way, and look how dark it is here, and how the hand shines against the black cloth" – he thought he was correcting the drawing; but I thought he was ruining it forever. He'd hand it back to me with a smile, as if he felt he was showing me the right way; and I'd look at those alien, sharp lines and my eyes would moisten: what a brutal scar running across the cheek, supposedly giving it a "more real" shape! What are those ghostly rings around the eyes? Where has all the grace and beauty gone? So what if the proportions are a little wrong? Where are the elegance and charm of the details, the precisely drawn lace edging and the wisps of hair?

Francisco:

He drew like a woman. For he grew more and more like a woman altogether; his arse went broad, like a wench's, wide enough to fuck, his voice had apparently broken, but didn't become manly; I know, although I'm deaf, because I asked Pepa – it seemed he just piped in a plaintive, feeble way, I could even see it in his eyes whenever he said something. Finally, to encourage him, I called out: "Hey you, with the broken whistle!" which didn't make him laugh at all, because he had grown so touchy about himself that no jokes ever amused him, especially ones aimed at him. He just crept about the house, with his nose eternally in a book, pale and unhealthy. "An embroidery hoop," I said, "that's what you need, the perfect thing for you!" He couldn't ride properly – he always sat on a mule or a horse like a sack, nor would he go to the bullfight – he avoided me, hid in corners, no doubt furtively flogging the bishop, growing paler and paler because of it.

Sometimes I would suddenly see him somewhere in the house, and I would wonder if he really was my son, the hope of my clan, the grandson of the gilder who, when necessary, became an ordinary peasant and worked his wife's land in Fuendetodos, the son of the painter who knew duchesses, some of them intimately, and the kings of a great empire, who allowed him to go hunting with them, to kiss their hand and remain on the most familiar terms possible. Did the heir, unfortunately the only heir to those two men have to be this weakling, this wench, this pippin, who at twenty years of age started to amass blubber here and there, who just fattened his arse, grew slothful, holed up in corners looking pale as the wall and never emitted the slightest squeak? How the bloody hell had it come to this? How had that lovely little boy, the finest sight in all Madrid, pupated into this pitiful drone?

Women, women were what he needed, to stop him from changing into one; but he never went to whores, nor did he care for young ladies of equal status to his own, or glance at those of higher status; I never saw his eyes light up. Not once, no, never at anyone. Or at anything either – as if there were some terrible parasite inside him, sucking out all his *joie de vivre*, all his masculine strength; I even wondered if some lecher had trapped him at school, got at him and turned him into a woman? Or a boy of his own age – something that sometimes happens between peers in a dark corner, and then grows, like a cancer, spreading its lethal venom right through their lives. I have heard of such cases, of men full of vigour, robust men, who were poisoned in their youth by this sort of villainy at school, and spent their whole lives burning with ardour for some wretched pup. Like goslings that mistake for a goose the first living creature they see on emerging from the shell, such men are only capable of associating the true pleasure of an embrace with the first person with whom they did it, fingering each other's cocks under the desk, stealing the key and hiding in the cellar, to couple like beasts on a mouldy straw mattress; oh, I have heard such stories about these men, who later had women, both whores and wives, who fathered children and were respectable husbands, fulfilling their marital tupping duties in an exemplary way, but who once in a while lost control, and went to see their spoiled friends, if you can call such scoundrels "friends", who drive the innocent to sin, and for years on end have committed the most hideous deeds, unable to free themselves of this burden, because the poison soaked into their flesh has bid them think they don't love their wife and all the women who have passed through their bed, but some boy, sitting in a dark corner under a pot hanging on the wall, frantically pulling his hood – even if for years that boy has been a man with hairy shoulders and a prick like a mule.

Was that the case? Who knows? I'm not a bloodhound, I never went up his arse, let alone inside his head, for how could I? Whatever he had in his head, it was nothing to do with me – but he was getting on for twenty, and when I saw how the boy was going to ruin, it broke my heart to pieces. Lying in her half of the bed, Pepa wrote me a note in the jotter that lay on the quilt: "Leave it be, don't go looking for a fifth leg on a cat, that's the way he is, that's how he was born. He always was a quiet child and he'll go on being quiet" – I don't think she ever wrote as much – "blessed are the quiet. Why do you insist on making a brute out of him like you?" – at this point she scratched me on the chest – "You've always been the same as well, I'm sure you have. Some people are one way, others are different, let Javier live in peace." Live – indeed I did want to let him live, I wanted to give him life, to pour life into him. But he found bullfights boring and disgusting, and he was ashamed to go to the bordello with me; if pinned to the wall, he said it was a sin and his confessor had forbidden it. "So heed your confessor, not your father, you drooping cock", I shouted, "a lot of good it'll do you"; I left the house, slammed the door and plodded off to the bordello on my own, but nothing went right for me that evening and I came home very quickly. "Pepa," I said, "we have to marry the boy off, or he'll waste away entirely." And she nodded and wrote down: "If we must, we must. But remember, Francisco, good wives don't grow on trees – first you have to look for one."

But what did she know? There was no need to make a special search – next day I wrote to Martín Goicoechea to ask if his Gumersinda was still eligible. Yes, she was. "Bottoms up!" I said to myself, and a month later we had the banns published.

Javier:

She was even pretty. Quiet. We came to visit, and I tried to make the best of it. I took a good look at her hair; it was thick and curly, brushed back and fluffed up over her brow. And her mouth. She had a pretty mouth. Plump lips, like something nice to touch and warm, like the pads on a cat's paws. We did not say much, because it had all been said for us as well.

Francisco:

Has this street, has this parish ever seen such a wedding? I doubt it. The Goicoecheas are rolling in money, they're in the business of money, for what else does a merchant do but buy and sell, buy and sell, conning simpletons in the process

– but as I could clearly see, the ceremony made a suitable impression on them too. And the splendour of our house made an even greater one.

The whole church was decorated, and there were so many pounds of candles that I prefer not to think about it – it was bright, as if you were sitting under the open sky, and there was twice as much incense as usual, to a point where some people were complaining of the dryness in their throats. In a dress she had been making for herself for the past few weeks, my Pepa sparkled with diamonds, and shone with gold; every movement she made produced a multitude of glittering lights, so that for this one day her ageing body seemed radiant. As if young.

As we walked in a procession from the church to the house, joyfully, the tears dripped from her eyes – well, I thought to myself, nothing can ever save this unfortunate woman. Nothing but weeping: sorrow prompted weeping, joy prompted weeping, it's every man for himself, because we're going to drown in it. At the house it was the same: the corks slid smoothly from the bottles, the servants did nothing but come and go, to and from the kitchen, the music played, and Pepa would most gladly have hidden away somewhere, shut herself in a wardrobe or a hiding place.

The guests sat on the patio at long tables, groaning with food, and I am not just being poetic – one of the tables really did come crashing down under the weight of a platter bearing a piglet. I looked and saw everyone suddenly turning around, because the noise must have been tremendous – about twelve plates alone were smashed to pieces – so I turned around too, and sure enough, the piglet was on the ground, the wine was trickling across the swirling tablecloth, a dog was leaping on the scattered sausages, in short, it was like a Flemish painting.

"Nothing's wrong," I said, "it has all broken for luck – good health and a long life to the bride and groom!" For you have to be open-handed, at least at a wedding.

Now and then someone came up and wrote me a note to say that he'd like me to give him a tour of the house. And I did not have to be asked a second time, especially as it was my cousins and friends making the request, who would not have the opportunity to visit us again and feast their eyes on my fortune in the near future – though in truth, some of them must have damaged their spleens as a result, but to hell with them. Ah, there was something carrying me along, shooting me into the air like a firework as I guided them through the rooms like that, breezily pointing to the paintings and casually dropping the names "Tiepolo", "Correggio" – I'd swear it meant nothing to most of them – and on, into the library, where the books, some still smelling of fresh printer's ink, were piled from floor to ceiling like in the palaces of the Duke and Duchess of Osuna, the Duchess of Alba, or the Count Floridablanca. I may not have read them all, but if the need should arise, I had the ancient poets to hand, the French tragedians and the Italian sonneteers; I had books about astronomy and metals, about medicine and painting, bah, even about bee-keeping. All that was simply ready and waiting for me, every single book like a *maja* with her legs spread wide.

I showed off the two gilded plates, on which the duchess had once sent Pepa some candied figs and roasted almonds, telling the messenger not to venture to bring them back again; then Pepa heard a rumour that Alba had sent us a pure gold dinner set for twelve people, and good, I thought to myself, let them talk, bugger the lot of them, may the devil fart in their faces!

Who is easier to run down behind his back than a deaf man?

But I was just as pleased by the ones who were delighted as by the ones who were jealous that I had so much property, and was giving it away so open-handedly to my son and daughter-in-law. I took a break, and looked out onto the patio through an open window: I looked at all those paws reaching for pieces of chicken, for bread, for bottles and glasses, I looked at all the beards dripping with sauce – what a sight! Isidro Weiss, the jeweller, who averted his gaze as they put more slices of duck onto his plate, was just as restrained as our late king – may he rest in peace – who was so ashamed of his greed that although he had specially hired a Neapolitan chocolatier and had a vessel kept in his chamber filled with a whole *almud* of steaming chocolate, whenever he signalled to have another cup poured for him, he averted his gaze, pretending he hadn't noticed anything, but then had to drink it out of politeness, so it wouldn't be wasted. That old aunt battling with a large artichoke is a veritable witch, ready to rip out a hanged man's tongue as a valuable ingredient for her magic brews. And that corpulent uncle, the Capuchin, isn't he just one big superfluous growth on a huge belly that never stops consuming? If they were served fried babies they would leap on them yet more eagerly, they wouldn't even blow on the hot ones to cool them down!

And yet – how am I any better than they, as I lap up all the admiration?

Javier:

I do not remember much of my wedding day – really only lying in bed that morning, when the whole house was already on its feet, my father's apprentices were setting up tables on the patio made of boards on trestles, the hired serving girls were crashing about in the kitchen with frying pans and pots, and I was afraid to open my eyes and come out to face this day, with all its pomp, and the finality of the choice which I had not actually made myself.

And after that I have nothing but disconnected impressions. a new frock coat, embroidered with posies of lily-of-the-valley, which my father had made for me by the tailor Herrero; it pinched me under the arms as I was tying my cravat. On my way down to the ground floor I passed a housemaid carrying two dead mice on a dustpan, shaken out of the traps. Nothing about the ceremony has stayed in my memory, absolutely nothing. Only the laden tables, the heat of the day, and the sweat trickling down my neck and soaking into my cravat. And the uneasy look on Gumersinda's face – poor wretch, she hardly ate a thing, for my frock coat was nothing compared with her corset. She pecked at her food, in the manner of a young lady from a good home: she'd take a tiny piece of meat and then chew it fifteen times on one side of her mouth, fifteen times on the other, then swallow it, have a sip of water, then take a tiny piece of aubergine, and again: chew fifteen times, another fifteen times, swallow...

The braying cousins, the bawdy jokes told aside, which didn't amuse me, but which disgusted me. And the next morning, when the sheet was put on public display, with a red stain that looked like a crushed insect. The next morning, which was the start of my adult life. God knows what on earth for.

Francisco:

A daughter-in-law in the house is like a guest in the house. You must receive her with open arms, entertain her, and not leave her in her room like a redundant piece of furniture. I thought the wedding would change something, but meanwhile that mute was just as silent afterwards as he was before; he went on floating from corner to corner, now reading a book for a while and putting it aside, now staring out of the window, now furtively drawing something on a sketchpad. All for nothing. And here was a young woman, frightened, not accustomed to this strange house – and with no help from anywhere. Her mother-in-law was not particularly fond of her, would talk to her out of necessity, but didn't drop in on her often. It was hard for her father-in-law to take care of the young one, toiling away from dawn till dusk for this little family, and on top of that deaf as a post, even if with a certain sense of humour and affection for the rather lost little girl. But what was I to do, as there was no other option? I entertained her. A real man will always find the time to sacrifice himself for the good of others.

A conversation with a deaf man is a monologue by the deaf man. What gets written down, even rapidly, even nervously, is just snatches – only one woman ever sat with me for hours, now listening to me, now jotting down long, convoluted sentences, full of jokes and puns, which I would then read out, either laughing or solemnly nodding my head. "You're nodding like an old mule, Paco," she would immediately write down for me. Later it was just "old mule", and we both knew what it meant; in the end even to elucidate a complicated matter she only needed a few mutually agreed signs and some comical post-scripts for decoration. But she is no longer alive – perhaps she drank cold orgeat with snow from Guadarramas and was cut down by a summer fever, or perhaps her doctor poisoned her on the orders of the court? Either way, she is decomposing in her tomb at the Missionary Fathers, and after three years there can have been nothing left of her but a skeleton covered in a torrent of black hair, turning red in the darkness.

So I spoke to Gumersinda, rather than read what she wrote for me, in a hand that in any case was too small and timid for me to be able to decipher it with the naked eye. I told her how in childhood, still in Fuendetodos, I drew a pig on the wall with an ordinary piece of charred stick, and the priest, who was carrying a sack of grain to the mill and just happened to be passing by, had stopped and given orders for me to be sent to drawing school in Zaragoza. Of course, I took that story from Vasari – I may be a country bumpkin, but I've done my reading – although that priest on his way to the mill, as if he couldn't send the housekeeper or a farmhand there, is my invention. The main thing is to tell a good story.

Javier:

Have you ever seen a black grouse making its display call, or perhaps rather a capercaillie? How it puffs itself up, ruffles its feathers, raises its head high, fans out its tail, and has no idea what is going on around it, because it is so focused on nothing but itself, not actually on some female who is essentially just there by accident? If you have, then you have seen my father.

VIII

He-Goat

Here, outside the circle, the most audible sound is the sermon; a bleat, though not monotonous, but rather ecstatic, fitful, finding it hard to hide its excitement; yet in a short while the ear starts to pick up a general rustling noise: it is thigh rubbing against thigh beneath the linen of pinafores and skirts.

Those who are sitting in the front row and do not have to display their hands folded in a god-fearing, or rather a godless way, are rummaging with fat fingers in the easily titillated crannies of the body, wriggling on the ground, straddling a rock and rubbing themselves against its rough surface; they are panting, groaning and moaning. They jostle each other, cast hateful glances at their neighbours and snort. Each of them knows that he has had them all: this one only once, that one many times, night after night, that one he caught in flight, threw off her broomstick and speared on his own broomstick, this one he pressed into the mud and hammered so hard in streams of rain that to this day she tingles at the mere memory, that one he rodded in a convent cell, another in a carnival procession – she just squealed under her mask as he lifted her skirt.

Each one dreams that he will set about her again, lift her legs and tickle her with his hairy groin – but they know they have become old and ugly, and he still has the same lust in him as then, and just as then, he only chooses the most comely young girls. He could reject them all, send his entire congregation to the four winds, but he prefers to torment them and tempt them, to bask in their insatiability, adoration and jealous strife.

Each of them dreams that one day she will attain peace, as the Rightful Spouse, enjoying respect, dressed in purest white, with a veil drawn over her eyes (so that she can pretend the He-Goat is faithful to her), and buried to the waist in rich earth (so that only moles, earthworms and blindly wandering roots should tickle her), as barren as a sterilized canvas.

Meanwhile their dreams make him keep growing, becoming blacker and blacker, puffing and fluffing himself up, and all for the very young postulant who is hiding her tiny hands in a muff as she tries to understand every "baa", every meaningful gurgle of his unbridled preaching; the black tulle of her veil shades her eyes, but he already knows what's his, he knows she is fixed on him. She alone, and way, way beyond there is nothing.

IX

Javier:

On our wedding day we were given the whole family house on Calle dos Reyes as our property – and although for some time yet my parents' things were being transported to their new house on Calle de Valverde, which on this occasion was being thoroughly renovated and adapted to my father's present position, we were on our own. But almost every day they would drop in on us at any hour, both together or singly. My mother came with gossip, alongside her a maid with a basket, and in the basket lemons, a guinea fowl or ripe melons. My father came smeared with paint, sweaty, straight from his studio. "I have come," he would say, "to stop you from languishing in total idleness here. All day at home! You should go and see a *zarzuela*, go on a picnic on the river Manzanares, or watch the regimental parade of Godoy the Sausage-Maker, instead of sitting about in stuffy rooms." He would make himself comfortable, without even waiting for us to write him a note on his pad; besides, sometimes he didn't take it out of his pocket: he only wanted to talk. Willing or not, Gumersinda would sit facing him and listen to this outpouring of words – unwillingly at first, but then more and more willingly.

What stories didn't he tell her! That in Rome he had lived at the house of a Pole, with a mad Italian, who drew ruins for money, and prisons for pleasure, and that for lack of cash he supported himself by being a street acrobat; through the Pole he met a mysterious Russian, a privy councillor at court, who begged him on his knees to follow him back to his frozen land, and there become the painter of blood-thirsty Russian tsars, who wore fur-trimmed cloth-of-gold and ate nothing but raw meat.

You had to hear him and see him, as he lounged in an armchair, as he made faces, clapped himself on his fat thighs, as he lit up at his own story, speaking louder and louder, on the edge of shouting, as he ignored me totally, not looking in my direction, sometimes for a whole hour – I checked with my watch in my hand – and as he used crude words which I would never have uttered in the company of a woman, least of all my own wife. There was no end to it. Nor did he ever let the opportunity slip to ridicule me, or to remind me that everything I had, I owed to him and him alone.

"So there I am, climbing to the very summit of the dome of Saint Peter's," he would say, "I'm bent double, like this, moving sideways, it's narrower and narrower, there's a precipice below – if anyone slipped, there'd be nothing left of him but a wet stain on the marble, but when a man's young, he's brave... not every man, perhaps – I can't imagine your sweet little dumpling exposing himself to such dangers... I doubt he'll ever go to Italy at all, though it wasn't for nothing that I sent the king all the plates for *Los Caprichos* in exchange for a lifetime annuity for my little Javier, thanks to which he can travel and educate himself as much as he likes... but never mind about that... I climb higher, a dove flies past, I dodge, a coin slips out of my pocket and falls from that height! It seems to fall for ever, and its jingle doesn't even reach me up there. As God is my witness! Ha, down there below some beggar is sure to have instantly regained the use of his legs and chased it half way across the cathedral. Good luck to you, I think to myself, go and drink half a pint to my health, that I might come down from here alive. At last I reach the very top, I take an etching needle out of my pocket and write underneath the dome: *Fran. Goya.* So, my dear, if you have ever wondered whose name is written at the highest point of the highest building in the entire Christian and pagan world, then I can modestly tell you: it is that of your father-in-law, who has painted a few pictures in his life, who gave you this house, and is now sitting here before you, happily drinking a cup of chocolate."

And soon after he's describing how he went to Rome with the *toreros*, who taught him the greatest secrets of the *corrida*, now he's lunging at a chair, telling me to pick it up and pretend to be a bull, so that he can demonstrate, with the poker in his hand, how he managed in the arena in the days of his youth. He will definitely not fail to mention yet again that at the age of four I was afraid of frogs, which led him to believe I would never be a *torero*. But a little later Gumersinda hears how he fell in love with a young nun and made a plan to abduct her from the convent – he even bought a decent rope for this purpose, and would have deceived the guards, climbed the stone walls and had his way, but the rope-maker's daughter turned out to be so lovely that he gave the nun a miss.

"Midnight? Indeed!" he said, feigning surprise when I wrote him a note to say that Gumersinda must be very tired by now and should have her rest, "so I've outstayed my welcome, children!" And he would get up from his chair, panting heavily, and glowering, as if I had broken the sacred rules of hospitality, and take his time leaving – only to appear again the next day and spin more of his yarns: about the proud Tirana, about dukes and duchesses, about carriages and hunting trips, about how many fieldfares he shot here, and how many hares there, and that in all Madrid to this day few can rival him in shooting from a distance of two hundred paces; there was no remedy for him.

Francisco:

Ha, I cannot say I am sorry when a pretty girl pays me attention and laughs at my jokes. And Gumersinda had the choice of her husband, a youngster – I will add that he was handsome too, for in those days he wasn't as fat, and was quite like me in my youth – and her father-in-law: an old codger, deaf and overworked, who had long since abandoned his *majo* costume and the joy of drinking in town until dawn, but did have that something in him which sets the juices flowing down women's legs. Why deny it? I knew she liked me, though it was all completely innocent, of course, I would never have had the audacity to break divine and human laws for some groping.

I simply felt plain, human sympathy for this very young, seventeen-year-old lass, virtually a child, who was shut up all day in a large house, with no entertainments, but with a taciturn husband. "Listen," I would say to him, sometimes even in her presence, to put him to shame, "whoever heard of a father-in-law showing more affection for his daughter-in-law that a husband for his wife?", and he would leave the room in a sulk. "It'll end up," I would joke, "with your first-born looking more like his grandfather than his father." And again he would pout and leave the room. I did what I could to relieve her. Out of the goodness of my heart. But I'd be lying if I said I didn't enjoy the feeling that if only I'd wanted, she'd have been mine in a matter of minutes. I would barely have entered the house, and at once she would be beaming all over, saying: "What shall I bring you, Father?", "What can I offer you, Father?", at once she'd be rushing up with chocolate, or heating some dinner, if I came from work hungry; she never called for the servant, but always brought everything herself. She was as good as gold, a treasure, not a girl, and that Javier of mine, shame to say, was such an oaf. It was just as well that he did eventually get her with child: her belly swelled, she became wayward, as pregnant women do, and grew even prettier. "Oho," I said, "the old biddies in Fuendetodos used to say that when a pregnant woman grows prettier, she's carrying a boy, and when she grows uglier, a girl. From that I deduce you're going to give me a grandson, not a granddaughter!" And she just smiled shyly – ah, pure sweetness!

Javier:

As soon as she fell pregnant, my father started appearing at our house not once, but twice a day – it's a wonder he still had time to do any painting. In fact he started staying at our house, and my mother did the same. They got their own permanent bedrooms, she had one, he had another separately, in another room he set up an easel, brought in some bolts of canvas, picture stretchers and pots full of pigments and paints – from then on we were never really going to be on our own. All so that he could bask in our warmth. He toadied, fawned, billed and cooed, and showed me even more plainly that I was simply in his way.

Only then did I start to understand his jokes that his grandson would be sure to take after his grandfather rather than his father, that unbearable confidence of his, that self-righteousness, and his affectionate way of placing his hand on Gumersinda's belly. How many times had there been when he'd come to pay us a visit, and I had instantly found something to do in town, just grabbed my hat on the run and vanished out of the door?

Hadn't he had plenty of opportunities, I suddenly realized, to lay his paws on her, use all his powers of persuasion, the tricks tried and tested time after time on models and duchesses, on townswomen and country girls? Those jokes, those glances, a knee pushed between the thighs?

And suddenly this terrible truth drove itself a path to the very centre of my heart, like a musket ball passing through the flesh of a watermelon, like the screw of the iron boots sinking into the feet of a *marran* under interrogation. Now I looked differently at every gesture he made, at every glance she cast, every night I agonized over why she didn't want to go to bed yet, and was listening to his ravings about bullfights, the habits of monarchs and the eccentricities of the Duchess of Alba – was it just a matter of politeness, or was there more to it? A bond between them, a romantic conspiracy?

But to whom could I confide these suspicions? Not even to myself, let alone someone else. Perhaps only the reeds on the riverbank, a rock, or a spoon. Patient objects. So I walked about the house, from room to room, not knowing what to do with myself; sometimes I spoke in a hushed tone to books and to stools, to the pillow and the candlestick. I wanted to go to the confessor – but can you confess another man's sins? At most you can confess the unfairness of your own suspicions. And yet I didn't know if they were unfair, or quite the opposite, as fair as could be. Neither the house, nor the city, nor the meadows and woods beyond town, where I would take off on long walks, none of them could explain anything to me – the summer was at its height, tumescent, everything was ripening and bearing fruit: grapes heavy with juice were falling into suntanned workers' baskets, the plums were bursting with juice, as if to spite me, and I, who had grown up in Madrid, had suddenly become a foreign visitor there, carried from place to place by the wind and my despair.

Meanwhile, her belly grew and something was ripening inside it which I was meant to love, somebody whom I was meant to love – but at the same time from day to day I felt a dislike towards this hard ball, towards this unnatural bulge, an aversion bordering on hatred; I would have been happy to peep inside there and check if it had its eyes from him or from me, black hair or chestnut, brows sharply raised or gently falling towards the corners of the eyes? I couldn't look at her, but nor could I tear my eyes away from the ever steeper curve of her belly. I wasn't talking to her, and she had stopped talking to me too – and again I agonized whether it was out of emotional sensitivity, or out of dislike for me and pangs of conscience that she had stained our bed sheets with the vilest version of betrayal, that she had soiled them with a foul deed?

Sometimes, for no particular reason, the blood would boil so much inside me that I would get up from the table in mid-word, bow to my wife and go outside, for otherwise the most hideous words would have come pouring from my lips like black pigswill, splashing the tablecloth and the dishes, putting out the candles with their stinking bile. At other times I thought she was being tender and sensitive towards me, but at once I would ask myself whether it was an ingenious game, designed to throw dust in my eyes? I was lost. I only found relief in counting the weeks and days until the birth.

At last the afternoon came when we sent in all haste for the midwife, and the manservant and I wrestled the old birthing chair down from the attic, which had come here once upon a time from Calle de Desengaño, but which afterwards, for obvious reasons, had never been removed to Calle de Valverde, and in which I had been born, as well as six of my brothers and sisters, later consumed by insatiable time.

I sat in the library, resting my feet on the firedogs by the cold hearth, and caught myself listening to Gumersinda's screams with a certain pleasure, until the thought made me feel ashamed, and at once I got down to reading again, but it was impossible. Neither the noise nor my racing thoughts would let me read in peace – besides, shortly after the maidservant came running in, shouting: "A son, a son, please sir, you have a son!" I leaped to my feet, overturning the chair, and raced upstairs. "My son," I cried, "show me my son!" The midwife handed me a bundle, a tiny parcel, in which there lay a child that was the spitting image not of me, but of my father.

"He's strangely like his grandfather," I said in a solemn tone, so meaningfully that Gumersinda opened one eye, "how curious..." "What's curious about it?" the midwife at once protested, as she straightened the pillows for child and mother. "Children are always more like their grandparents than their parents. You can always see that, well, unless someone else has fired a shot from a side-angle!" She laughed out loud, making an indecent gesture away from me, so I didn't see it properly. "I've delivered some of those, oh yes, indeed I have. You should be glad you can see a family resemblance, because even if it's to the grandfather, a resemblance is always a guarantee that the little one is the flesh of your flesh, the blood of your blood."

That was no consolation to me at all.

Francisco:

I do not know, I simply don't get it: how can a man be quite so indifferent to the birth of his first son? On the day my Antonio was born, first I danced in the streets with joy, and later I got so drunk that I didn't come home for two days because I hadn't the power in my legs. But he was like a cold fish: he came in, asked why the child was so unlike him, and left.

How could anyone not be thrilled with those little black eyes, those tiny fingerlets, the down on his skin, the tiny feet like little jewels? I went as soft as butter. That very day, when I belatedly ran to Calle de los Reyes and, jumping two steps at a time like a youngster, climbed to the first floor, I knew a little person had come into the world whom I loved no less than my own son.

When I came out of Gumersinda's bedroom, I saw Javier sitting in the library, entirely in the dark (the dusk was already falling and the shadows were thickening), as if not joy, but tragedy had befallen him. I stood in the doorway and gazed at him, as he gazed out of the window – I even wanted to go in and say something to him, but I didn't know what. How hard it is to understand your own children.

X

Javier:

And it has happened: I enter the room and I see the two of them, sleeping – his old body, sagging here and there, uncovered, because it is the middle of the day, the air is still, and only thin stripes of light coming through the shutters slice across that broad, matted, he-wolf's chest, with bristling black-and-grey shaggy fur, soft and dough-like; a drunken Noah, with more on his conscience than inventing wine. And I see her, small, slender, golden-skinned, lying next to him as if she had accidentally fallen there, accidentally naked: she just caught a foot while trying to straighten the picture above the bed, and overturned, feeling faint, and now she's lying, curled up, beneath his left armpit, and the streak of light that is cutting across his chest runs onwards, across her cheek, and lands on her slanting neck, where it illuminates a small armada of droplets of sweat; they are lying almost separately, but actually together, with the bedclothes kicked to the foot of the bed, and they are only touching knees: a small, girlish knee, too large, like a horse's, for such a fine leg, and a big, gnarled knee, which with its twin holds up that powerful, stocky body, that in a single day is capable of shooting several birds and hares, devouring four large meals, drinking a quart of hot chocolate, painting half a portrait, doing a dozen drawings and also feeling another body, one that differs from his own in terms of its protuberances and orifices; at least one such body a day.

So I seize whatever I have to hand. A knife, a pistol, a rapier – each time something different. And in an instant I decide to slash their throats, first one, then the other, so that they'll wake up, choking, spurting thick, viscous blood in all directions; they'll seize at their own necks, trying to stem this river, but this river will be impossible to stem; fully awake, they'll look first at me, then around them, in horror, growing weaker and weaker, until they collapse on the very spot where they were lying together in repulsive sin; or not, no – one goes back to the bed, and the other, let's say it's her, let her get out of the bedding, let her scramble out, place one foot on the floor, and reach out a hand in my direction, not quite cursing and not quite begging for forgiveness – only then does she crash to the ground with a loud thump. Or the rapier – a sharp thrust straight into the heart. There's also a lot of blood, but they can still talk; bah, if someone's strong – and there are those who don't lack strength – he can lunge towards the window and shout: "Murder, help, murder! My own son has raised a parricidal hand against me". With a rapier, should have been added; I would never have acted with my hand alone. Finally the pistol – here at least the whole thing would soon be over; worse that I am a very poor shot, and now I can see the drama changing into a farce; a bullet in the bedstead, him jumping out of bed with something swinging between his legs, shielding himself with a chair, throwing a bowl seized from the table, the next bullet landing in some stupid spot, in his forearm, ear, or toe, laboriously finishing him off, the servants coming rushing from downstairs and pounding on the locked door, my mother dragged out of bed, where she had just been having her far more proper siesta. No, that I did not need – I preferred the directness of the knife or the rapier.

I imagined it hundreds of times. As I ate breakfast and

supper with them. During mass in church, during the sermon, only stopping for the elevation; at a picnic, whenever I saw the old man tearing apart an orange with his thumbs, handing half each to my mother and to Gumersinda, and at that same moment I would see him splashing fountains of blood onto his easel standing by the bed (I don't know why; it never did stand there) and onto what would turn out to be his picture – unusually, a failure. He would say: "Why is our dumpling sitting there so quietly?", and I'd smile and shrug, while at the same time unhurriedly observing, with scholarly care, the twenty-three large dagger blows now turning blue, with which I had nailed him twenty-three times to the mattress, to which he had earlier nailed Gumersinda with an entirely different tool – that too, painfully injured, had its place in this revolting scene.

But the convenient solutions brought by daydreams rarely ever become reality; what wonderful proof – two people lying *in flagrante* in my parents' conjugal bed or in mine, or on any other litter, couch, or heap of hay – what a luxury that would be, a real gift from fate. But what did I have? Nothing, guesses; other mental images – poorly lit scenes against dark backgrounds, where a barely visible, slight young woman, whose reddish hair can only be seen in the gloom thanks to its golden lights, rolls in the folds of graphite-grey sheets (at night, white takes on the colour of graphite or dull basalt) with a large, whitish body, overgrown with coarse bristles. Who could have called those recurring dreams proof, those images that kept appearing before my eyes at any time of day or night? If I were to rid myself of them, it was only by imagining something even stronger: a bloodbath in the bedroom, sticking the rapier in and pulling it out of his body, out of both bodies, or wiping my knife on the edge of the sheet.

Francisco:

That boy has gone terribly sour. Terribly! There's not a squeak out of him. He could have a chat – he won't, he could go for a walk – he doesn't, he hardly budges from his armchair to nod to me in greeting. He should go out, I tell Gumersinda, for some entertainment – he should go hunting, see a bit of the world, have something good to eat away from Madrid, where everything is rather heavy and lies on the stomach... or is that old age? Once I used to eat an entire chicken, drink a whole bottle, and on top of that a piece of chorizo cooked in white wine, some fruit, pâté, a couple of glasses of strong drink from Jerez, and I could still party, dance or frolic the night away. But now just a few slices of ham and I feel so heavy I have to take a nap. It's quite different when I'm out hunting with Martín... ah, then I eat for two, and the two of us together eat for four – clearly the fresh air is good for me; perhaps I should finally do as the grand gentlemen do, put aside a few pennies and buy myself something on the banks of the Manzanares, grow fruit and plant vegetables for myself, like my father and my father's father?

Javier:

What was born grew. At least that is how I explain it now, because there are many years of my life of which I remember nothing or almost nothing. I know that Mariano was little, but I do not remember either his wail, or his face, only the long, empty days that passed me by in idleness. I would get up, put on the clothes made ready by the servant, for if I had to choose them myself the day would end before I could ever manage to make all those decisions; I ate without appetite, but without distress either, as if I were washing or putting on my shoes: just another thing in the course of the day that had to be moved from the "to do" column to the "done" column.

I would encounter Gumersinda. And I could see how she was changing – more slowly than the child... yes, it's curious that I can remember the speed at which he pupated from a newborn to an infant, from an infant to a toddler, from a toddler into a little boy, and so on, but I cannot remember his successive faces, except perhaps for the frozen one I know from his portrait, and which now appears to me as his real face for all those years; Gumersinda was slowly, but just as irrevocably changing, in the same way as I was too. Her lips were becoming less pink, her face was losing its girlish freshness – yes, I know, the comparison with a flower seems obvious, but I would prefer to avoid that; let us keep our dignity. Her thighs swelled and grew broader and softer, like dough rising on a pastry board, covered with a cloth to stop it from drying out. I wouldn't say this sight made me feel disgusted, but nor did I have any need for it.

Sometimes I thought I didn't understand a thing, and she was innocent. At other times I thought I knew perfectly well what was going on, and that she just dressed in the robes of innocence; on those days I couldn't look at her. I was unable to resolve it, I didn't want to try.

My mother was gradually becoming an old woman. She kept repeating the same gossip over and over again, went up the stairs with a greater effort than in the past, and less and less often felt like going to the marketplace with her maid and bringing us melons or plucked geese. My father was gaining fame – he had long since painted a large portrait of the king and his entire family, as well as all the rest of his wanted and unwanted relatives: the queen's lover, the bloated Godoy the Sausage-Maker, as the Prince of Peace of course, lolling about on the battlefield in the "war of the oranges", his unfortunate wife, the pale Countess de Chinchón, but also – for balance – his mistress, Pepita Tudo, and did it twice: once clothed and once naked, so that at the push of a special button one canvas moved aside, revealing the other, so in an almost magical way Godoy could undress his nymph whenever the fancy took him...

I didn't give a damn about any of it.

Francisco:

When the Sausage-Maker banned the *corrida*, I said I'd give all the money I got from him, down to the last *maravedí*, for his cock to droop every time he saw Pepita naked... what a joy it was to hear that when the rebels announced the end of his government, he spent a day and a half sitting like a fat mouse under a pile of old carpets, without a drop of water, and nothing to eat but a single thin slice of bread that he'd seized from a table laid for supper!

I didn't yet know that was just the beginning.

Javier:

Of course I remember that a couple of years after my wedding there was a rebellion, the heir to the throne turned against his parents, Godoy had to escape, and the French marched into the city... but I didn't give a damn. I would get up, wash, dress, eat, go for a walk, return home and go to bed. My real life had shifted entirely into books – there I lived through countless adventures and emotions, I fell in love and I suffered, I swam across oceans and fought against sorcerers, I captured fortified cities and wept over the fate of wretched women taken captive by the Saracens. I have extremely colourful memories of it. But apart from books, a total void stretched away before me: all those days were just one long and uninteresting day.

Meanwhile, my father was in his element. He rushed about the city in search of all manner of abomination and feasted his eyes on it, stuffed his head full of it, just as a beggar crams food into his toothless mouth: quickly, greedily, out of hunger and out of the fear that someone will take it off him; he went all the way to Zaragoza to make copper engravings afterwards of disembowelled houses and disembowelled women, and that lone girl, Agustina, who climbed onto the bastion over the corpses of the defenders, among whom lay her lover, and lit the fuse of a cannon; he painted her portrait – the French and the Poles slashed it with their sabres when they entered the city, along with the other paintings they found in General Palafox's quarters. But here too he kept flying out of the house like a spat-out pip, whenever he learned there had been a bloody incident; on the second of May he was disconsolate after being late reaching the Puerta del Sol and had seen nothing, just a skirmish of little significance not far from our house; but on the night of the third, wrapped in a mantle, he took a lantern, ran to the execution site and drew the corpses, live, so to speak, at once, still warm. That seemed to me low and vile, as if he had only dragged himself there to gorge his eyes on the blood, the excreta flowing from their bellies, the odour of fresh corpses. Whereas I chose what seemed to me pleasant to look at: soldiers, ours or foreign ones, standing in pairs or threesomes outside our gateway, clean uniforms, curled moustaches. Not that I lacked patriotism – I loved Spain with all my heart, and with all my heart I hated the French; but

what has that to do with uniforms in the sunshine? Bah, my
first real picture arose out of this excitement, this elation, out
of a patriotic poem that I read one afternoon in a small book
with a green marbled cover. *The Prophecy of the Pyrenees* by
Juan Bautista Arriaza. A thing of beauty.

> *Ved, que sobre una cumbre*
> *De aquel anfitëatro cavernoso,*
> *Del sol de ocaso á la encendida lumbre*
> *Descubre alzado un pálido Coloso,*
> *Que eran los Pirinéos*
> *Basa humilde á sus miembros gigantëos.*[1*]

And at once I saw it, the whole picture, the details too, as
if it had appeared to me on the pages of the book: from the
chaotic smoke and clouds wreathing the noble Colossus, via
his muscular arms and shoulders, right through to the panic-
stricken flight of the French troops – horses, mules, carts and
little tin soldiers. For years nothing had excited me, until
here suddenly I was so overwhelmed by this vision, which
demanded immediate recording, this image existing nowhere
outside my head, that it almost took my breath away; I got up,
went over – I remember it perfectly – to the window, went
back; then it carried me into the next room; I didn't know what
to do with myself until I had dug a large empty canvas out of
a corner, primed for the portrait of some French colonel whom
my father had been meant to paint, but who had been sent
to another city, killed on the way and, reportedly, butchered.
My father had taken most of his canvases, almost his entire

[1*]   Look, upon the summit of that cavernous amphitheatre,/flooded with
light by the setting sun/a pale Colossus discovers his prize/what were once
the Pyrenees/reduced to humble stumps when compared with his gigantic
limbs.

supply, to Zaragoza and donated them to make dressings for the defenders of the city; all that was left in Madrid was what he had already managed to paint on, if only partly, and which couldn't be used to bandage wounds.

Of course, despite my haste I preserved a minimum of decorum: first I took off my frock coat and hung it on the back of a clean chair, took my watch out of my waistcoat pocket and put it on a table so it wouldn't fall out, took off my waistcoat, untied my cravat, rolled up my shirt sleeves, neatly, so they wouldn't be crumpled, and after putting on a smock, I threw myself into a wild frenzy of painting. I could hear Gumersinda calling me through the closed door, but I was so captivated by what I had seen in a sudden, dark flash, as I read Arriaza's poem, that I was unable to answer her, to shout a reply – as I hastily mixed the paints, laying a sombre, stormy sky across the breadth of the canvas, then the shadows on the muscles, the drab greens of the landscape – to say that I was in the studio, that I was painting; afterwards I heard her bustling about and talking to the servants, but as if from far away, as if from another time, for here, in front of me, on a canvas measuring more than four feet by four feet, this vast shape was emerging – no, not the giant, but the entire vision, in colour, almost in motion; how great was her surprise as she came up the stairs for the sheets and heard the easel being moved, then flung the door open, and saw her lawful husband half undressed, in nothing but his shirt and smock, painting a picture. Had she been expecting someone else to be there, someone who wasn't at home just then, but who stood at that easel for hours on end, day after day, as long as he wasn't out hunting, eating, or chasing after some woman? I don't know. But on seeing me, she raised a hand to her lips and, as if unwittingly, showed me the key to the linen cupboard, after which, quite simply, she turned on her heel and left.

And I went on working, and for the first time in my life I felt I really was painting – I threw myself into bed tired as a water carrier, sweaty, sticky, my hands still smeared with paint, although I did my best to paint as cleanly and neatly as possible; the giant had sucked all the strength out of me – I created him, but not out of nothing: out of some vital energy, which made him grow in strength and me weaken.

Next day I didn't bother to dress properly, I just threw on my shirt and smock and rushed to the studio; I merely told Gumersinda to come and fetch my clothes from yesterday, so I wouldn't stain them as I stormed about behind the easel. A couple of my brushes had gone completely crusty – for like a sloven I had collapsed into bed without cleaning up after myself; but others could be saved, and now, using alternately wide brushes and ones that were as thin as twigs, I brought the Colossus out of the darkness. The successive layers of paint gradually shaped his large, athletic body, making its immense muscles rounder and fuller, and giving it three dimensions; on the one hand the coppery, oily glints on the tanned skin, on the other the dark shadows and tangled locks on his head; a son of the earth, in his primordial strength, he rises higher than the peaks of the Pyrenees and shows the little Frenchies who's going to rule whom, who's going to crush whom, and who's not going to act above his station.

At noon my father, who was working somewhere in the city, sent his assistant, Asensio Juliá, to fetch him a little sienna, turpentine and linseed oil – Juliá came in, nodded to me and set about searching the drawers and examining the shelves; but suddenly in all this rummaging about he looked up, as if he had only just realized that I was painting. Javier Goya, the butt of everybody's jokes, the painter who had never painted a single picture, was standing at the easel in a smock, and on a canvas four by four and a bit feet was not so much painting, as forging an enormous monument, creating a giant, which was stirring such panic among the Grande Armée that he didn't even have to turn his great face towards those little tin soldiers, he didn't have to sweep them away with an iron hand or blow them off; all it took was his presence, his back as broad as a mountain range, his fist as large as a house full of fury.

XI

Francisco:

"Your son is painting," Juliá wrote for me on a slip of paper.
And I said to him: "What are you drivelling on about, Little
Fisherman?" – because we used to call him El Pescadoret,
after his father, a fisherman. And he wrote: "I'm not drivelling,
he's painting." "What?" I asked. For what on earth could he
paint? Well, what? So I asked myself what he could paint,
that idler who lay on his belly all day like an old woman, and
whose entire labour consisted of turning the pages of books.
"Go and see," wrote Juliá. So I had them take me to the Calle
de los Reyes. I bang on the door, and a new serving girl opens
it to me and jabbers something. I ask: "Where's the master?"
So she does some more muttering and refuses to let me in – I
came close to feeling her up in the doorway. But there was
no time, so I just grabbed her by the arm, very close to her
pap, and said: "I am the master's father, now show me where
the master is instead of talking, because I can't abide prattling
females!" So she shut up and showed me that he was in the
studio. Up I ran, jumping two steps at a time – there's still
vim in my calves and my loins – I go in, and indeed, there
he is, the scoundrel, standing at the easel. He shuddered, I
saw that, but he's pretending he hasn't noticed me, as if he's
concentrating. Good, let it be so. I creep up, sideways, as it
were, and yes indeed, the son of a bitch is painting. He's close

Jacek Dehnel

to finishing. A bit of an imitation of me, the colours will do, the horses are terrible, but never mind. He never did have a talent for animals, and in truth neither did I; I could knock off any portrait, but at the thought of an equestrian portrait I broke into a sweat. If the king had told me to paint the entire family on horseback, I think I'd have died of apoplexy; one horse is too much, in any case nothing about it fits, it has a rump like a ball and a skinny head, its legs grow out of nowhere – a real curse. I'm looking and looking, the whole time he can see me, and knows he can't go on pretending he hasn't seen me, so he shows that he can in fact see me. As if he's surprised. And he makes gestures to show it. So I look, I squint, I make a face and I say: "Eeh, eeh, yees..."

Javier:

We were both standing there. One of me was painting the galloping troops, mixing paints on the palette, adding a drop of this, a drop of that, sprinkling on more vermilion and sienna, casting floccules of cloud onto the Colossus's coppery skin, seeing to everything that still needed to be done; the other I was in a completely different scene, though on the same spot, acting out a series of gestures and words in my head. I saw my father come in, with a smile on his face, for he had already been told his failure of a son had embarked on a large work and was painting a colossus defending heroic Spain against the invader. I was acting it out in my head like a theatrical scene, without end: he walks up to the easel, his eyes become as big as saucers, and there are tears in those eyes. Tears of emotion. "Son," he says, "you are painting!" As if he were saying to his miraculously healed child: "Son, you are walking!" Whatever had been taken from me, I had now obtained, whatever had

81

been held against me, was now forgiven me. And I saw him dipping a brush in paint, just as the king dipped a brush in scarlet and painted a cross onto Velázquez's black tunic, which he had once told me about and depicted in an unsuccessful engraving that he had decided not to print – and just like the king, he writes in the bottom, right-hand corner "1J". Javier's first picture. Once again: "1J". Javier's first picture. Once again: "1J". Javier's first picture. And once again. And again.

Francisco:

A grown man does not need mollycoddling, so I just muttered something and said I had come for another bottle of turpentine, which El Pescadoret had forgotten.

Javier:

He didn't say a word, he just mumbled and grumbled under his breath, took the turpentine he had come for, and that was all I saw of him. From the stairs came the sound of him loudly saying: "Goodbye, Gumersinda!", for they must have passed each other, and then the rattle of the carriage outside. He had gone to paint. His great works. His famous pictures.

Francisco:

On my way out I met Gumersinda on the stairs, who looked startled, with her coiffure in a mess; I leaned towards her, until a strand of her hair tickled my nose, and I said I'd be back late that night, when Javier was snoozing; that she was to wait up without fail and let me in – a man of my age can't stand at the door for long in the middle of a cold night. She waited up and let me in. "Javier threw himself into bed the instant you left," she said, "I am afraid he may be sick, in a fever – his eyes are burning". I smiled, and said to her: "Well, girl, that's normal – you've married an artist, and the devil burns in an artist, in an old one and a young one alike. Even if he looks a bit, you know, half-baked." I took two large candelabras from the dining room, lit the candles, shut myself in the studio and gave orders not to be disturbed, unless the young one awoke; I looked around for a place to dive in case of need, set down the candelabras right beside the easel and looked.

Oh, the son of a bitch. He was a dark horse – as if nothing were going on, as if it were all nice and smooth, like dinner at the bishop's. But here he was showing his talons. The face, the nose – not quite, but the hair, those greasy locks – superb. The fist seemed to have too many bones, it was too rounded, but the elbow – superb. The horses, as you would expect. Although some would still come out. Come out alive. But the boldness of that dark triangle in the bottom right-hand corner, its contrast with the small figures – brilliant. The little trees in the distance were not so good, a bit like mushrooms. And the clouds, the cannon smoke, through which you could see that gleaming, muscular body… he must have had a drawing of the Farnese Hercules to hand… ah, those openings in the sky are superb! Superb. I couldn't see properly, so I started removing the candles from their holder and fixing them to my hat. There you are. I like the fact that he's standing with his back to us. Who knows, what is it – strength? But a sort of suffering too, that moment when the strongman tenses his muscles, like the blinded Samson, whose hair has grown back and who is just about to revenge himself on his enemies, those Phili-whatnots. I like that, that's really something. And how about that bold streak, the shadow between the clouds, running from the shoulder to the edge? No smoothing, no distressing, just real, virile painting! The animals are a little too ranked, too even. But as a whole – well, well. We shall paint the ceilings of the Escorial together yet!

But the black horse on the left is really… just a moment – I reached for the palette, mixed a little ochre, a little navy blue, a little bone-black, and corrected the strange hump for him. There. And a touch more.

Javier:

The next day I slept until late – when I opened my eyes I saw Gumersinda leaning over me, alarmed, with a look on her face as if she were just about to become a widow, escorting her child dressed in black to his father's grave. "What is it?" I asked. And, as if coming to, she buttoned her lip, stood up and said: "Nothing. It's long past noon and you're still tossing in bed, wasting the whole day." She turned, flung back her dress and left the chamber, slamming the door.

For the last few days I had leaped up at dawn, as soon as there was light for painting – as if I could sense it through my skin, as if the rooster were living inside me, crowing at dawn "Jaaaaviee-e-er, Jaaaaviee-e-er," dragging me to the easel like a rag doll, freezing cold, with barely anything tossed on my naked body. Straight to the pots of brushes, oils and turpentine, to mix the colours, stand back from the canvas and approach it again. But now I felt nothing. I dressed fully, and once in my frock coat I went to the studio. A picture like any other. Nothing special. I merely examined the black horse in the left-hand corner – how could I have let something like that slip? I just rolled up my sleeves and, taking care not to drip paint on my clothes, I corrected the horse, which looked strangely flat.

There. And a touch more.

Indeed, I put the picture aside for some time to let it dry properly. I sometimes came to look and see if the impasto were cracking. When the right time came – and I also questioned Asensio – I varnished it. And there he stood on the easel, God knows what for, like a reproach. Even if I was on my way from one floor to another, having a game of cards in the evening or playing with the child, I knew he was there, with all his latent strength in those giant muscles, which even so had proved insufficient. Finally, unable to live with him under the same roof, I had him packed up and sent to my father on Valverde Street. When he came back the messenger said: "He bid me wish you good health, sir." Good health. Let's not try to be funny.

Mariano:

My father? He painted? I remember something from childhood, I must have been literally a few years old – we went to my grandparents' house and I was allowed to enter the studio, on condition I didn't touch anything. I had no intention of touching anything at all – I was wearing a lovely black costume with a turndown lace collar and I was afraid of getting it dirty, because everyone kept saying I looked like a little prince. And I was afraid that if I tore a leg of my breeches or touched something dirty – and everything was dirty in there – they'd stop saying that. Grandfather told me to sit on a chair, but I showed him it was spattered with something, and I was wearing clean clothes. He laughed awfully and went to fetch a clean chair; he also set a music stand in front of me. "Because you like to sing," he said. And I had to sit there without moving, but there was nothing interesting around me, just some bits of rubbish and old pictures. One with a naked man. But I was afraid to ask Grandfather what sort of picture it was, and in any case I didn't know how to show it to him – only when Grandmother came with chocolate, Grandfather's in a cup, mine in a simple mug so I wouldn't break it, I asked her what the picture was of. And she told me in a sort of warm voice that Papa painted it, because Papa is a painter too. I was awfully surprised, but just then I saw the portrait of me, in which I was wearing the hat that I had left in the hall, but which wasn't on my head at all.

"You can't do that," I said, "it's cheating." And I left the room, but everyone laughed a great deal at that. And they smacked their lips in wonder because I was so like the other Mariano, the Mariano in the false hat.

XII

The Three Moirai

The flood of life spreads far and wide: out it pours, milky in the light of the full moon, in between the forested hills, seeming boundless and free; in spring it spills abroad, in autumn it heads rapidly for the delta of multifarious endings.

But this murmur, this low murmur, is not the murmur of water, or the murmur of leaves in the robust plumes of branches – it is the fast running of a pliant, living thread, writhing a little like an earthworm, like a vein pulsating with blood; running through ancient fingers, horny at the edges and smooth where thread after thread keeps flowing through them, relentlessly.

No one can see their faces, they perform their tricks

behind our backs, but they are certainly repulsive: old age and ruthlessness have changed them from women into sexless, grey-and-brown effigies with large noses, hairy nostrils and balding brows that cast shadows on their rheumy eyes. And the fingers? Look at those lumpy, gnarled, peasant fingers, for digging the earth and spreading manure, not for doing fine manual work: spinning, measuring and cutting off human life. Oh, what hands you have fallen into, dear soul – soiled and calloused. There you sit, wrapped in some rag, with your own hands tied behind your back; you can only swing your left foot a bit, or bat an eyelid – not much. For that is the extent of your free will – you are not a sailor, but a piece of cork, carried wherever the waves may wish.

You are fed on nonsense about witches charming away illness, curdling the milk in cow's udders, or laying eggs covered in cabalistic symbols. About witches soaring high above the world of the god-fearing, bending over the human earth, about witches smearing themselves with fat from a hanged man and mounting broomsticks or pitchforks – but there are no worse, there are no other witches than these: Clotho, Lachesis, and Atropos. One clutches a skein wound around a small figure – yes, that is you, that is you, dear soul, *animula*, *vagula*, *blandula* – and rapidly unreels twist after twist. The second uses a small plaything, a snake swallowing its own tail, to measure off the successive cycles: spring-summer-autumn-winter, spring-summer-autumn-winter, and once again, and once again, but she wrinkles her bald brow, for something is telling her there are too many of these revolutions. The third grows impatient, now and then snapping her black scissors, which grate from congealed blood. Snip-snap, snip-snap.

Tied up, carried to an unknown place above the river's luminous floodplain, all you can feel is the pulsation in your wrists, bound with the pulsating thread of life: that is your blood tapping on the wall of that blood.

XIII

Javier:

"I am not sick at all," I said yet again, "I simply want to sleep and rest." But Gumersinda kept summoning doctor after doctor, who examined me, nodding their heads, asked stupid questions with pained looks on their faces, sniffed my urine and inspected it in the light, took my pulse, applied leeches and told me to swallow herbs. But I was not sick. Quite simply, in the twenty-fifth year of my life, I felt I was not a man at all, but a wooden marionette, and the strings tied to my arms, elbows, hands, knees and feet, to my eyelids and lips, had been cut and were lying on the floor like long, lifeless strands of hair. Marionettes with cut strings are useless – they are shut away in boxes and buried. Or at least put aside on a shelf, where they can lie in peace, undisturbed by marionettes dressed in the black attire of doctors, or by one especially insistent marionette in a lady's dress and by the rather battered figure of an old boar, which creeps into the house and sniffs about in search of what it likes best, its delicacies, its truffles: decay, death, and disease.

My mother came to see me too. But she hardly said a word to me: she understood. She had been buried her entire life. Like a female mole, burrowing corridors in the rich earth, bearing and miscarrying a succession of young, interring them as soon as they went cold, and seeking the best roots for her husband the inseminator. I took her as my example. I covered my head with a pillow, turned my face to the wall and said to myself: look. To spend thirty-five years like a bean pinned down by a rock, only putting out white shoots, blindly seeking the light and the air. To be a lady, the wife of a rich man, and to spend thirty-five years like a servant, indulging the master in everything, absolutely everything, and yet always mattering less than bullfighting, less than the *sainetes*, less than some old friend from school, with whom he exchanges countless letters, less than the models, less than the dressed-up ladies, less than the pictures, less than the entire rest of the world. What mattered less than she did? A rat that ran across the courtyard, a leaf? Some spilled water, a tuft of cat hair?

She would sit on my bed and gaze at me in silence. I would turn away from the wall, slowly. A marionette with cut strings does nothing quickly – it hasn't the strength for that. I placed the pillow, which before then I had been using to cover my face, beneath my head, opened my eyes wide and looked into hers, and it was as if we were pouring black earth from eye socket into eye socket, full of pebbles, the larvae of beetles, rootlets, sticky clumps of clay and swollen grass seeds, from eye to eye, without a word, without end.

Mariano:

Papa was sick. Not like Grandfather, who couldn't hear anything, so I had to ask Mama to write down what I wanted to say to him on a piece of paper, or like Grandmother, when she stayed in her room, which she wouldn't let anyone enter, apart from the maid with a tisane, or like me, when I had to stay at home, lie in bed like a stone and drink elderberry juice to make me sweat. His body was healthy, it wasn't burning with fever, it wasn't throbbing, it wasn't aching, it wasn't shot through with pain from any part of it. But to me it seemed as if he was in another bit of the world, and had just left his body here with us, with a remnant of life in it, only enough for the simplest functions.

I never knew him any other way, so I couldn't see anything strange about it.

Only when I found out that other children did not have such dormant fathers did I realize there was something in life that I simply didn't have – but I also learned that many children have no fathers at all – theirs had had to flee from Madrid, or were killed by the French, or on the contrary, by the patriots because they were *afrancesados* who, for instance, had received medals from Pepe Botella (we little boys never spoke of him otherwise, unless the teacher was asking, who in any case must also have called him "Botella" at home, and not "His Majesty, Our Gracious King Joseph I of Spain"): I had two schoolmates whose fathers were *josefinos*, and they were probably not spared any of the hurts that one seven-year-old can inflict on another in the school playground.

But there were more interesting things than my sick father. Corpses lying in the streets. And fights for bread and beans, beggars snapping up food handed out by the Franciscans. Sticks, fingers and stones all went into action – we could see everything from the school windows, but the teacher watched to make sure we were looking at our notebooks.

Francisco:

I remember the moment: I am standing behind the easel, finishing off some white lace against the background of a velvet doublet, I look into those eyes like coals and say to myself: it has survived. The Goya clan has grown stronger, has begotten the next generation – almost all branches of my tree have died out, and the only one remaining is rather lopsided and not all there, yet it has put out a lovely bud, so lovely that sometimes I wonder if it wasn't I who sired this brave boy in a drunken moment. How much innate refinement he has, how much natural gentility! And despite the fact that he gilded the main altar in Zaragoza Cathedral, sometimes walked behind the oxen when necessary, and ploughed the fields like Cincinnatus, my father was a thoroughbred nobleman, with his roots deeply embedded in the hard Basque ground, and my mother came from the *hidalgos* – I wasn't born a nobody. In truth we are not called Goya but de Goya, which was proved by the archivists long ago – all that rummaging in old documents cost a bit, but a man doesn't have money only to economize on the splendours of his clan.

Javier:

He came to the house with some documents, records, and charts; I almost dozed off over my cup of chocolate. I had a foggy memory of him showing me all this before, when I hadn't yet reached table height. I cast an eye at it, and wrote him a note: "Do you remember the *Capricho* with the donkey?" "Which one?" he said, pretending he didn't know what I meant. "Lots of them had donkeys..." "The donkey in a frock coat," I wrote, "with a book in its front hoofs, where there are drawings of its ancestors, nothing but donkeys? *And So Was His Grandfather* – I think that was the title." "Bugger all you know," he replied, and gathered up the papers, "bugger all you know, it's a real wonder my son has gone to the dogs so badly."

Saturn

Mariano:

Grandfather says that I am Mariano de Goya and I am to walk with my head held high. He says that even when you lower your head to look at a mouse or a lizard, you can still have it raised the whole time, inside you.

Javier:

Perhaps if I had had to get out of bed and dress, to prevent Mariano and Gumersinda from starving to death, like so many people in Madrid and all over Spain, gathered up each morning from the streets, from hallways and their own beds, thrown onto two-wheel carts, and then piled off the carts into communal graves, I would have got up, put on my shirt and breeches, shoes and frock coat, and gone to some job. But I did not have to. Even lying belly up, I had enough from the duchess's legacy, from the royal annuity for unsold sets and plates of *Los Caprichos* and from monthly "bonuses" from my father that we could run the house to almost the same standard as before the war; even during the worst famine there is always someone willing to sell his piece of bread, his last beetroot or bag of peas. We could even afford to hire Gumersinda's cousin to help with Marianito; her husband, Isidro Weiss, the corpulent Jewish jeweller, had dismissed her for immoral conduct – one day the thought occurred to me that perhaps that would cure me. To grab hold of such a woman – knowing she was no lady of virtue, for the jeweller hadn't thrown her out of the house for being innocent – pin her to the wall, lift her skirt... I imagined it in detail, then lay in bed and wondered what had got into me? The same evil spirit that sat in the old man? Afterwards I saw her almost every day, as she went about the house, biting an apple, with her little boy in her arms – the older one had stayed with the father, the younger must have been sired in another man's bed – and the very thought that I might have touched her made me feel unwell. A poor, browbeaten woman who would have nothing to feed her little one, if Gumersinda had not yielded to the persuasions of my parents and taken pity on her.

But all this happened as if behind a door, in another room, in which the entire rest of the world existed. I was sliding across the surface of life, across the surface of the war as across a frozen pond, passing day after day rapidly and without unnecessary effort. Being myself was quite tiring enough for me to be able to have any other occupation.

When I felt a little better, I did some looking. I'd make a note for myself, sometimes I'd tear the pages from the sketchbook, sometimes I left them there: in it, words mixed with pictures, with nervous drawings of the most ordinary objects; even a salt cellar, if drawn the right way, can seem horrified by the world.

I did not touch any brushes – I felt disgusted by them. By the paints too. They revolted me like congealed blood, like scattered shinbones, like chopped-off fingers.

Whereas the old donkey was flourishing. And painting incessantly.

Francisco:

It is not a painter's job to appoint a king, to divide up wealth, to exercise power, or to head armies – his power is inconspicuous and limits itself to a few feet of whitewashed canvas, on which he paints those mightier than himself: witches and generals, satans and magnates, in whose hands he is a docile plaything. Some might throw him into jail, shut him in the spiked interior of an iron maiden, sentence him and burn him, others might smother him in temptations, infect him with the foulest diseases, take away his will to live, suck the strength out of his loins, stifle his child in his wife's womb, or reverse his good fortune.

You may laugh at the dungeons of the Inquisition, at the shouting generals, and at the old wives' tales about witches, but do not be surprised when this laughter leads you onto treacherous ground. Better to light the dukes' candles and the witches' wicks, but just occasionally, for your own peace of mind, blacken the regime and the sorcerers in a cunning manner, so that Evil might not discover what you mean by it.

Javier:

Did he paint the old cuckold king, his debauched, hawk-like wife, and Godoy, the well-stuffed Sausage-Maker, sprawling on the rocks? He did. And did he paint the new king Ferdinand, who drove out that entire company and sat on the throne? Just the once? Did he go to Zaragoza, give away canvas for lint, and paint a portrait of the heroic defender, Palafox? He did indeed. But he accepted a medal from the French kinglet. After which on the night of May the third he scurried up the hill to sketch the still warm bodies of the executed men, just because it might come in handy. And it did. When he was later commissioned to paint four pictures about the uprising, those drawings were the perfect thing. He also painted Wellington, like Palafox, on horseback, what's more, on top of the still wet Bonaparte – and the only thing that linked the portraits of the old queen, the British general and the Zaragozan duke was that in each case the horse was a disaster. Gold braid, sashes, faces, breasts under muslin, the neck of a plucked guinea fowl... all these he painted faultlessly. But every horse he painted was like an oversized dog.

Another portrait of King Dotella was ordered by a deputy from Peru, who became a councillor in Madrid; my father turned up his nose a bit, but when he learned that Bonaparte and his entire court were leaving for Andalusia and he would not be appearing at his studio in person, he had himself brought a print of his portrait, and spruced it up in a trice inside a medallion, and put whatever you may wish above and below the medallion: angels, Glory blowing a trumpet, Victory with a golden garland, a girl in a crown as an allegory of Madrid with a coat-of-arms on a shining shield, in short: all that tinsel and trumpery so loved by all the small people who suck at the teat of power.

But hardly had Wellington captured Madrid than the old badger pasted over Bonaparte and wrote the word *Constitución* inside the medallion. He was too quick, because Bonaparte came straight back and had to be painted in again – he had the luck to find a print of the portrait somewhere, buried in a pile of old paper for lighting the fire. Only a couple of months later, Wellington crushed the French sot at the battle of Vitoria, so the old man told a stripling from the studio, Dionisio, to paint out Joseph and put the *Constitución* back in again. Hardly had Ferdinand returned to Spain and overthrown the Constitution than he had to cover up the inscription. Finally there was a toad-like Ferdinand in there, but apparently they're having to redo something again now.

XIV

Javier:

He seemed to me to be getting weaker – he had been deaf since long ago, but gradually he started to lose his sight too, and to squint as he leaned over a copper plate, closely watching the motion of the etching needle. Doctor Arrieta made it plain to me that it wouldn't be long now. How wrong he was.

He did more and more griping, in fact it was incessant – even my mother lost patience with him. She would come to see me, in the corner room where I used to sit for whole days on end, neatly attired or slovenly, in an old dressing gown, and launch into her litany of complaints about my idleness, about illness, about life in this house being like life in a convent, but at the same time, from underneath it all, hints of weariness and hesitancy broke through. She never attacked my father directly, but his outbursts of rage, his unfaithfulness and constant grudges against the entire world were well known to all.

Only once did I hear a real grievance from her; I had come to Calle de Valverde, my father wasn't there, he had gone on a hunting trip, or maybe he was painting somewhere outside Madrid; she was on her second day of the spring cleaning. Yes, it must have been during the spring cleaning, because only then, once a year, did my father agree to his studio being cleaned, though even so you could hear his angry grunts, curses and shrieks for a couple of days after his return when he couldn't find some brush or etching needle; in fact, it was always hard to find anything in that mess, but after spring cleaning he had someone to blame it on. We were standing in the corridor, by the door into the studio, watching as the maid swept out the dust from in there, the lumps of paint, strips of rag and white powder, which rose from the floor in small cloudlets.

"All because of this," muttered my mother, "because of this white powder." I glanced at her and asked: "What's that? All what?" And she smoothed a wrinkle from her sleeve and replied: "Well, everything. The little ones' burials, the miscarriages. Your frailty. And other things I don't even want to think about. My brother, your uncle Francisco, knew all about it; he was indeed an artist, but he was interested in chemistry, he brought home books, from France even, and explained it to me, and to your father too, he wrote it down for him on bits of paper, because in those days already... it was after he came back from Cadiz, miraculously cured, but deaf... Except that he never did anything about it. Lead white and cinnabar. The cinnabar was only ever in the equivalent of medicinal quantities, but the white, how much of that white came in, *arroba* after *arroba*! You can no longer remember how your father used to work on tapestry designs for the king – those were large canvases, six ells wide by four, by five, various sizes; three lads were hired to stretch them, glue, prime and sand them, prime them again, then sand them again... There was powder everywhere, on the shelves in the parlour, inside the drawers, in the kitchen on saucepans and frying pans hanging on the wall, between the plates standing in the dresser, everywhere, everywhere. It went through the corridors and the rooms, it lay wherever it liked, it got into your eyes, your hair, and up your nose, from dawn to dusk you could smell it. At the time I thought it was just another nuisance of living under the same roof as an artist, and in fact I was used to that – when you have three brothers who are painters, you can put up with a painter husband too. Only later did my brother tell me it was poison, and that people die of *saturnismo* because of it... He told me to throw away all the copper pots in which the solder had worn through, and to hang a wet cloth in the doorway of the studio, but how would your father ever agree to a wet cloth in the doorway, can you imagine? Anyway, he wasn't working on the tapestries any more, he'd grown bored of those cheerful little scenes with dances, parasols and taverns, he didn't need such enormous canvases any more."

She said this as if she were telling me about a troublesome servant from years ago, or about a piece of furniture that squeaked in spite of repairs, a small inconvenience of daily life. And only at the end did her voice falter, when she said: "The house is a woman's grave. But does it have to be a grave for almost all her children?" – and she seized me by the hand. Me, the only one who had survived the sanding of the canvases by three hired lads.

Francisco:

I never had a life that was idle or empty – always working like a Trojan for my living, I never had the time for fun and games. I had no illusions: life is like a painful enema. And yet, as I approached seventy, I realized that whole years had run through my fingers, while I did everything for others, and never had any time for myself, for my own joys; if I went away on a hunting trip, at once I had to come back to paint the portrait of some countess in need of a good poking; as soon as I had pinned a wench to the wall, at once I had to get on with the painting, because the house costs money, the chamberlain is being insistent, and even if she doesn't say anything straight out, Pepa is waiting for six yards of brocade for a new dress. My back is aching, I'm pissing one drop at a time, but dog-eared old Paco takes hold of the cart again and pulls, because he has always done the pulling, ever since he was little, since he was a stripling: one school, another school, portraits, tapestries, colour not like that, composition not like that, the dress hasn't come out ornate enough, the face isn't pretty enough, though in real life it's such an ugly mug that I feel like a grave-robbing thief who has opened a coffin and is staring at a rotting corpse... but never mind, I go on painting, I make alterations, I bow and scrape and hold out my hand for some chink; behind my left ear there's one leech, behind my right ear there's another, and there are more of them just waiting to latch on. Never mind, old Paco is cut from decent, well-tanned leather, he isn't worn out yet. But if you're going to stop old leather from shrivelling up or crumbling to dust, you have to take care of it, you have to polish it and oil it. And nothing does it as much good as a nice bit of puppy fat.

And that's just what she was: not overweight, not saggy, but padded with pleasant puppy fat here and there, where a woman should have a sweet little roll of it; she had a bottom like a pear, paps like apples, a cunny like a little plum – she was a fruit-seller's basket, not a woman! I could bite, suck, and lick her until the juice was dripping down my chin, until I could taste the sweetness on my palate... sin is sin, but let's admit it: is it really so hard to detect the Hand of God in all this? What were the chances of a rotten old stump, sixty-plus, deaf, lustful perhaps, a womanizer – but let's not fool ourselves, ugly too, for what could be attractive about this swollen, ample body, the white bristles on this chest, this ever receding brow, these ever more drooping lips? – and so what were the chances of an old fart capturing the affections of a lovely, lovely girl, a very young married woman thrown out of the house by her husband, who went crawling from brothel to brothel, and had entirely squandered her nice, decent dowry, and now had the audacity to reproach her for a moment of forgetfulness? What were the chances that this orphan girl brought up in a convent, this terrified little dove, would change at my touch into a she-cat on heat, that she would straddle me, writhe underneath me, scratch me on the back and beg for more? O you stupid fat jeweller! No whore in all Madrid can give you what you had right under your very nose! What were the chances of her having to seek protection and finding it with us, with Gumersinda and Javier, but also with Pepa, and with me, of us clothing and feeding her, of us taking care of her Guillermino, and her taking care of our Marianito, and everyone being pleased and happy? I ask you, can anything evil possibly result from two people, a desperate, ill-treated girl and a life-worn man who works like an ox, finding happiness together, without doing anyone harm – for what's the harm in it for her vile husband? That sort of harm would be a noble deed, but is that toad capable of caring about anything apart from his own rotten little shop full of gold rings? Or for my dear, forbearing Pepa, who understands perfectly that after almost forty years it is not healthy tupping, but incest? Who in their right mind – and I'm not talking about sex-starved old clerics with wilted little cocks, for they've got everything in a hash already – could see Satan, rather than God at work in this?

And how wonderfully she takes care of my Marianito! When she comes to see us with him – for how much time could anyone spend in that house of mildew and despondency? – the four of us are like a new family, like the first people after the

Flood, populating these ravaged lands again: one babe in her arms, another holding her skirt, I paint, she cooks up goodies for me with her own fair hands, while Pepa sits in her room and doesn't pester us. Can you imagine a happier old age than having a new start in life?

Javier:

I remember very little, so even that I see blurred, as if through fog: interrupted scenes, isolated conversations. I no longer know what I noticed first: the envy and dislike with which Gumersinda began to speak of her cousin, her peer, with whom she had spent so many pleasant times in childhood, and who until now had apparently taken such splendid care of Marianito? My father's elation? The fact that suddenly he almost entirely stopped coming to visit us, and if he did, it was only for half an hour, at best an hour, most of which time he spent with Leocadia, and then took her off to Calle de Valverde, saying he had "great need of her there, and she's sure to be happy to help Pepa"? Or perhaps it was that my mother became even quieter, even greyer, even more invisible, a shadow of herself from years ago, when she was strong, fertile, and stood firmly on the ground? Maybe it was the new confidence with which Leocadia, until now intimidated and afraid of her own shadow, began to voice her opinion, whether asked or not, on any topic at all; maybe it was the first quarrel, when she felt strong support behind her, or maybe the fact that this small, though stocky little figure, crowned with rampant ringlets cascading onto her shoulders, who until now had generally kept to the kitchen and the nursery, began to make more and more frequent appearances in the main rooms, stretching out on sofas and in armchairs, and adopting alluring poses with a little book "exquisitely" positioned in her hand, a finger between the pages, which she did not read; and also that one was more likely to see her dressing up than taking care of the little boy? I don't know.

But I do know that it was she who killed my mother.

Francisco:

At this age every man should be prepared for what the good Lord has allotted us. That was what Pepa believed. She had chosen herself a place at San Martín's, and we had written a joint will – she was buried just as she wished, in a tertiary's habit, without pomp. In any case, who would have thought of pomp in such times – wondering how many candles and what sort of ornaments to have on the catafalque, when Wellington was standing at the gates? According to the testament, we ordered twenty masses for the salvation of her soul, and some other money went on buying back prisoners and charitable deeds in the Holy Land. If anyone had asked me, it was like pouring money down the drain, but so be it, if it mattered to her.

A couple of days later Javier and I went to the notary, don Lopez de Salazar, and shared out the property. Everything was inventoried as necessary, every last pair of my drawers was entered in the register. So be it. The leech sucked up his half, but I made sure he choked on all those objects: candlesticks, mirrors, a tin bath, eighteen of these chairs, twenty-eight of those, eight footstools, trays, cups, books, everything, everything. I parted with my prints by Rembrandt, and Piranesi – I once lived with him in Rome in a single room, a dreadful slob he was – two Tiepolos, two Velázquezs, a Correggio; a great many of my things, including a few splendid ones. I also told him to write down *The Colossus*, so he would know I value it no less than my own paintings. He was even tempted by *Alba*. Tough. I took cash: these are turbulent times, and I can't put the house on Calle de Valverde in a moneybag, but one-hundred-and-forty-thousand-six-hundred and twenty seven *reales* – indeed I can. And the bloated fool is welcome to stay behind with all that he laid his paws on, let him watch as army after army smashes up the wardrobes and tips the last of the silver knives out of the drawers, let him watch as they shit on his books and slash his pictures with their broadswords. I will be far away with every one of my *reales*. And with a beautiful young woman at my side.

Javier:

Mama departed this life just as she had lived it: she gave way. She closed the coffin lid behind her just as she used to close the door of the room behind her whenever my father was screaming that he couldn't concentrate on his painting with her walking about the house; but this time she took revenge on him. I don't know how she forced a will like that one on him – whether she said out straight: either you sign it, or this very day I'll throw that harlot of yours out of the house, and she will never cross the threshold of any of our houses again as long as I am alive, neither here, nor on Calle de los Reyes? Maybe she didn't have to. Maybe it spoke for itself. Do with her as you wish, but our joint money goes to our joint son, not to some bastards. Remember that you came to ask for my hand as naked as a Turkish saint, and that my dowry, which wasn't such a large one either, was enough to turn the head of a simple fellow from Fuendetodos like you, my Paco. Sign here, and no more talking – I've dipped the pen in ink for you myself.

There, that's it. Or maybe it was simply that, when he agreed to it, he was only thinking about that woman's bare arse in bed, and not what "half the property" really meant? I don't know.

I took it all from him without so much as batting an eyelid. House, furniture, library, pictures. He had the cheek to give me my own *Colossus* as if it belonged to him! But never mind about that: he was left with nothing but cash, which he'll never take out of the city anyway, because they'll confiscate it from him at the tollbooth, so even if he did want to flee from Madrid, he'd have to leave almost everything with me. He let himself be fooled like a child.

Francisco:

The longer I live, the more I appreciate my deafness. Even if Leocadia starts to rant about something, I can always close my eyes and cut myself off from her completely; let her bang the pots together in the kitchen, let her scream, let her throw whatever she wants – I will be left all by myself with my arthritic hand, trying to make it draw a line: the only correct one amid countless incorrect ones. Small children shout – I remember how that used to drive me into a frenzy at the old house on Calle de Desengaño, where instead of stone walls there were thin partitions, and the nursery adjoined the studio – Leocadia's children are perfectly quiet. The war is quiet. They can shoot somebody right outside my door, a man whose knees have been shattered by a cannon ball can beg for help, he can wheeze and howl all day and all night – I won't hear the shot, or the prolonged wailing, I will be sleeping like a baby. If of course a baby can have dreams like mine. But not even deafness can protect you from dreaming. In my dreams I can hear every snap of a twig beneath a witch's foot as she steals along to the sabbath with a basket of newborn infants, I can hear the flapping of the human bat's papery wings, every note of the soldier's hoarse scream as he is speared on a fence stake, and the laughter of the idiot giant. From that there is no escape; it is this country howling inside me.

Javier:

If someone had told me I would behave like this I would have laughed at him and upbraided him as a fool – I said to myself, and wrapped my coat tighter around me, for there was a cruel wind blowing, carrying sand along the streets, bits of rubble and the stench of war, not diminished in the slightest by the heaps of flowers that greeted Wellington. And yet I went. I told myself that when robbers or stray soldiers from some defeated regiment drag him out of the carriage in the middle of nowhere, when they slit Leocadia's throat, smash the children's heads against a wheel hub, split him open from belly to collarbone and leave him like that, dying, as they walk away with the moneybags full of *reales*, I'll be sorry about that half of the inheritance. But this wasn't to do with the inheritance. It was about something that I couldn't explain to myself: so there I was, walking along, whistling a tune. And the whistling was helping me to keep walking.

Francisco:

I've always said it: the caricaturists did not invent the idea that gendarmes are ugly and stupid; the ones who appeared at our place in the middle of the night, screaming, banging their rifle butts against the door and getting everybody on their feet – though I shouldn't actually complain about it, because it was only Leocadia who woke me, tugging me first by the arm, and then, for lack of reaction, by the ear – they looked as if they'd come straight from the worst caricatures on earth. And the sort drawn by an unskilled hand: a botch-up of a drawing, a garish colour scheme; a provincial artist, and after a pint or two.

What could we do? Indeed, the trunks were packed and ready for the road, indeed we did not have permission to leave the city. Who had informed on us? Who was it? I don't know. The maid, the washerwoman, Leocadia's husband? Informers are as common as dogs, they vie to race each other to every new regime, with the *maravedís* still jingling in their pockets from their predecessors, who bent an ear to their whispering.

XV

Pilgrims

Far spreads the darkness that has covered the world, far it spreads, and densely; you toil your way through it laboriously, your feet bogged down ankle-deep in putrescent black; churned up, the black splashes, clouds steeped in black move across the dark sky like heaps of blotting paper, heavy with ink, used to dry letters bringing the worst possible news.

And yet on they go, endlessly; their long procession has no beginning, it comes from all directions, from in among the mountains, from all portals of the city, from the gates of old mansions and from the doors of houses, from convents and courtyards; at first they drag along separately, but the further they get, the more of them there are, and the more they unite, huddle together, and stick to one another. The monk in the cowl beside the madman with a stick, the balding thinker with the down-turned mouth, looking humbly and searchingly all at once, and right alongside the happily singing musician from the *sainetes*, with his mouth open so wide you could throw a blood orange into it. Tramps and old beggarmen, secret police in capes and top hats and a *maja* in a widow's mantilla, which she will willingly cast off, should the opportunity arise.

A shaft of light picks them out of the darkness, and they herd together, uncertain whether to run from the excess of brilliance and grandeur, or to be brave and walk onwards, all the way up to his majesty himself.

The city is sick, infected by mildew and typhus, by ten plagues, by anger and despair, as foreign troops keep changing place in it by turns like streams of cockroaches in different coloured carapaces – meanwhile here, on the Manzanares, in San Isidro, there emanates the source of light of the very first brightness, to which they are drawn like mindless moths.

Only once they are an arm's length away do they realize that what is shining, what is flooding them with brilliance, is a monster. That can be read in their eyes, which are so round. Even then some of them cannot see it.

XVI

Javier:

A succession of different armies came trailing across the scorched soil, among fields sown with ergot-infected grain, the blood soaked into the sand, as if trying to reach the centre of the earth, and down our little street, then across the Bridge of Segovia coach after coach drove by; and a succession of grand ladies rode past in carriages with tightly-curtained windows, from behind which not so much as a bow or a lock of hair was showing, not even the flash of a single diamond brooch.

Nothing had the power to knock the self-satisfaction out of him. He regained the post of royal painter, and did a vast series of etchings showing bullfights, day in day out he drew something. If he wasn't drawing, he went into the garden and gave orders to old Felipe, who in any case wasn't yet so old then; after that he would walk down the avenues of fruit trees to the raspberry bushes and the artichokes, raise their twigs, press and kiss them.

Enamoured of a Turnip – an ass bent double to bow before a vegetable. Nothing and no one could move him. Some zealous fellow accused him of collaborating with the French, because at Pepe Botella's command he had helped them to remove the most valuable works of art from the royal collections, which were later sent to the insatiable little runt in Paris – he easily got himself off the hook, saying that apart from a few

111

masterpieces which the invaders had identified anyway, he had fetched out the worst trash from the cellars and attics. Someone else reported that he'd got an "aubergine" from Botella – he had, but he never wore it; he procured a letter from the parish priest and a few witnesses, and it was plain sailing. Some petty bureaucrat at the main storehouse for sequestered items dug up some paintings taken from Godoy's palace and rushed off to the Privy Chamber of the Inquisition to say that such and such had painted a naked woman – they were even going to summon him before an Inquisition tribunal, but nothing happened. The whole matter blew over. After all, there were four of his paintings hanging on the triumphal arch through which the king had ridden into Madrid. And although this new king couldn't bear him – a feeling that was mutual – the salary of the first royal painter continued to flow in an uninterrupted stream. Not much was demanded of him either; he did knock off a gigantic canvas portraying the Junta of the Philippines, in which the carpet and wall are more interesting than the faces of the king and his officials, but who else had always worked at court, painting boring ceremonies and ministers in tail coats, on which every last thread of gold braid is visible? Even so he had plenty of clients – Englishmen came, and Frenchmen. They asked to be shown his paintings, and he would puff and swell, fluff up and have them bring out canvases old and new, never sparing himself the compliments. There wasn't a good word he wouldn't have said about himself.

All these processions passed before my eyes as in a dream: the room outside the studio was refurnished to be an anti-chamber, a place for quiet, reverent conversations. As if standing behind the easel there were not a repulsive old man, drooling over a young woman and impregnating her, all sweaty and deaf as a post, but a saviour, a magus to whom one comes for advice.

He knew how to win the admiration of absolutely everyone, without exception. Can you imagine anything more detestable?

Francisco:

Madrid is not a city for an old person. If you don't break your leg on the holes in the cobblestones you'll slip on a heap of rubbish; no one does any cleaning here, the abbey of San Antonio just lets its pigs run wild, and they rummage in the piles of rotting refuse, or are startled by the rumble of a carriage and race blindly down the streets, knocking over pedestrians. In summer everything is scorched as if in a frying pan, in winter you're ankle deep in mud and filth. And you only need a trip to the banks of the Manzanares, like all the grand gentlemen, and at once you can enjoy the fresh air, shoot a quail or a hare, even from the drawing-room window if it comes up close to nibble shoots in the kitchen garden. The king himself, Charles IV, may he rest in peace, said about me: "That dauber has an even greater passion for hunting than I do!" That places me under an obligation.

Little Ladybird will have somewhere to frolic, she can wander about the garden, lay her little head in the shade, and instead of the urban stench and dust she can breathe in the scent of mown grass and ripe cherries... Why didn't I think of uprooting myself from the city before now and buying some inexpensive, modest place? Finally, at this age I have the right to relax in peace and only appear at court when I really am required; the king has no need to economize on messengers. And anyone who wants a portrait by Goya can make a little bit of an effort to come just across the Bridge of Segovia, where the hermitage of the Guardian Angel used to be – a hermitage is the perfect thing for a recluse like me. Twenty-eight *fanegas* of arable land, a garden, a house that may not be large but is comfortable, easily big enough for the three of us, myself, Leocadia and little Rosario, and when Javier and Gumersinda come with Marianito from the city there will be somewhere for them to stay the night... there are two wells, one in the courtyard, the other in the vegetable garden, which is pretty big too – what more could one expect for sixty thousand? Life going on all around you, shoots sprouting, fruits ripening – I can gaze at them for hours on end... Haven't I always said I have three masters: Velázquez, Rembrandt, and Mother Nature. I have Velázquez in the royal collections and Rembrandt in etchings, but I only had Nature when I went out hunting with Martín. Now I'll have her right under my nose, right under my great big conk, which I'll use to sniff out all her secret scents.

And there's the name too: the House of the Deaf Man. It fits like a glove. When he and I met at the notary's to sign the contracts, there we stood opposite each other, understanding every detail, every wrinkle of the faces fixed one on the other. Two deaf old men – he a peasant, and I a painter, but in view of our deafness we were entirely equal; that was evident from the speed with which we read off the notary's questions, written in our notebooks; all we needed were the first few letters of each word.

Javier:

All the boundaries of shamelessness have been overstepped – sometimes I am glad my mother did not live to see this. How that woman lords it about the house, how much at home she feels. How slimy they both are – the way the old man looks at her as she swings her hips, the way she strokes the bristles growing on his ears – it's revolting. If not for Gumersinda's insistence that we have to visit them on the Manzanares to give Marianito somewhere to run about outside, and to let us all "have a nice time with Father-in-law", I would never have set foot there. But I prefer to agree to an outing to the riverside with baskets of food than to quarrel the entire week about more or less the same thing.

And so we "have a nice time". We are given rooms; the local brick, fired in the sunshine, has a particular odour, which drives me to distraction. When it's heated up, the smell is even stronger, so I open the windows to get rid of it, but the wind carries not just the dark aroma of earth, grass and rushes in from the fields, but also the stink of the bricks, which they use to build everything around here: houses, garden walls and chapels.

The old man is behaving like a youngster in love; his life is nothing but plans for the future. He has hired a gardener on a permanent basis and has built a cottage for him, as if he didn't believe that at his age anything he plants will only produce fruit once he is already six feet under in a wooden box. Whenever he says: "We're planting those pear trees for your Marianito, they're his favourites!" I am convinced that deep in his soul he believes that rubbing himself against the young body of the jeweller's wife will eventually give him back his youth, and he'll gorge himself on those pears yet.

I watch him go hunting with his gun, supervise the digging of ditches and the planting of vines, I watch him tend the artichokes and tell us all to eat them and praise them for growing so immense. He has changed into a character from *Los Caprichos*; I spend days on end just thinking up titles for endless caricatures which he himself would never have drawn, of course, or etched with a fine line onto copper plates.

I Adore Your Grey Hair: this one shows a fat old badger clambering on top of a fleshy *maja*, who is stroking the grey wisps of hair on his back with one hand, while reaching for a knife to deprive him of his purse with the other.

A donkey in a tumbledown little stable: *My Kingdom*. No, that's poor.

A smith forging chains which are binding his feet and growing longer and longer, link by link: *The Industrious Man*.

Or a *maja* with the snout of a sow, and an old man with a sweaty nape staring at her, his belly spilling from his breeches: *That's Love In Her Eyes!* Good title? I'll find a better one.

I work on these etchings day and night. I think it all through, from the layout of the grey and the black right through to the tiniest scratches of cross-hatching deep in the shadows. I just never sit down at a table with a copper plate in one hand and an etching needle in the other. I have no need of that – it's enough that I can see each of these compositions as I lean out of the window, trying not to notice the smell of burning brick, and consider a patch of white or black; disengaged from this house, from the garden and from the lascivious old man, if only in this small sphere, I am free.

Mariano:

With Grandfather I am never bored. He doesn't make me read. He tells me stories about famous bullfights from the days when he was still young and all the girls were in love with him. We go hunting together and he teaches me to shoot – he says I've got his eye, and that although nowadays he can't hit the target as well as he once could, he'll soon teach me how, and once again Goya will be the best shot in Madrid.

Sometimes we walk about the garden and we make fun

of Papa, but Grandfather has banned me from repeating that to others, especially in front of Papa, so I do not repeat it; but whenever we go to the countryside there's always a lot of laughter.

I wish Grandfather was my father, and Papa was a stranger whom you pass in the square and think: what a sad man, it's better to finish off someone like that so he doesn't have to go on suffering.

Francisco:

This time it was a close thing. I was mired in a sticky mess, but Doctor Arrieta pulled me out of it by the ears. Fever robed in yellow, but with black vomiting, and right behind the fever its old friend, the Reaper. Prepare for the worst, old man, I told myself, you're never going to roust in this vale of tears again, you'll never draw another line, you'll never plant another artichoke. But they cured me. I lay in bed, wrapped in my overcoat, under my red counterpane, for just a moment earlier I had been shivering with cold, but now I was sweating like a pig, and I told myself: that's enough. I vowed that if only I recovered I would pull myself up by the bootstraps and go as far as possible away from this accursed corner of the world.

In my delirium once again I saw everything that had wound its way before my eyes in the past few years, and things I hadn't seen too: slashed-open bodies, ravening demons, convicts rotting alive in the dungeons of the Inquisition... not much more and I'd have been stuck in there with them, manacled in irons, far away from all that I love. By a miracle I got off the hook, by a miracle I was cured, but there won't be a third miracle.

As I was painting a thanksgiving offering for the doctor,

gazing in the mirror and imagining what my face might have looked like consumed by fever, as I was mixing paints on my palette, endeavouring to find the right shade of pasty pallor, just then beneath my windows the liberals were being led to the gallows; another day I set the shutter ajar because I needed more light to work, and I saw the French marching below again, brought in to quell del Riego's revolt. Leocadia was a bundle of nerves because her older son, barely thirteen, had joined the rebels – what else could he have done? Schoolboys and students cannot go to lectures in any case without obtaining a certificate of anti-liberal conduct. Some fools had torn a notice-board from the walls with the articles of the Constitution carved on it and had smashed it to pieces, and apparently in the streets they were singing: "Long live fetters, Long live oppression, Long live King Ferdinand, Death to the Nation!" The king, who had only just been forced to flee from Madrid, came back again, and at once began to confer new titles: Marquis of Loyalty, Marquis of Fidelity, Marquis of Constancy. Apparently he was brought in on a triumphal chariot dragged by twenty-four young men – since that time there has been a lot of pulling and dragging on the Spanish streets. They say del Riego was not shot dead: he was put in a basket, with a green cap on his head, and dragged through the streets behind a donkey's rear, until finally he was disembowelled. El Empecinado, the Castilian swaggerer, vanquisher of the French troops, whom I painted not so long ago in a brick-red jacket with gold braiding, that sincere moustachio, was imprisoned in an iron cage at Roa – as he was led to the gallows he tried to break free, but tripped on the hem of his winding sheet and fell to the ground. They pulled him by the neck until he gave up the ghost. Squads of soldiers are going about the houses destroying all illegal books – either French, or printed when the Constitution was in force.

Why be surprised, if the king, his brother and his uncle, held captive in Talleyrand's castle, apparently kept going to the library merely in order to hunt down obscenities and tear them from the covers or slash the books with knives. When they set about burning Voltaire and Rousseau, they almost sent the entire library up in smoke; instead of reading they preferred to pray and embroider a gown for the Virgin Mary in the chapel – so it's no surprise they have this sort of little helper nowadays. Fortunately we took everything worth reading to the house on the Manzanares, and left nothing but boring books in Madrid. Who would want to take all that out and burn it? Well, but if you can be made a marquis for that? Others have founded a secret society, of the Exterminating Angel, and they are tracking down anyone who has, had, or could have dissenting views. Leocadia saw a man having his sideburns and whiskers torn off in the marketplace for carrying a yellow handkerchief – then he was led about, bleeding, with a cow's bell around his neck; another woman was shaved to the quick, then tarred and feathered for wearing a yellow ribbon. Ripoll the schoolmaster was hanged for not going to Sunday mass; they placed a flaming barrel beneath the scaffold as a reminder of the good old days of burning at the stake. I try not to think about it, I try to follow the movement of the etching needle. But even there I can see them all, reflected in the shining orange copper.

Javier:

Gumersinda was the first to find out that Leocadia had finally taken Guillermo and Rosario and fled with them across the Pyrenees – I don't know how she did it, but before the moth-eaten old bear had rolled in by coach from the Quinta del Sordo, I already knew from her that from now on he would be sitting there entirely alone, not counting Felipe and the latest cook (they all left in turn because they couldn't bear the master's moods and the mistress's scenes); he just dusted off the sleeves of his overcoat, sat down heavily in an armchair and said: "Call Marianito. I must transfer the house to his name so they won't snap it up if I am arrested. They won't take anything away from a seventeen-year-old boy for the sins of his grandfather. Let them think all I possess is the clothes on my back, and a few old brushes."

Mariano:

I thought I should be sad and show him sympathy; I was given the house, but I knew I was only getting it on paper, and I was less pleased about it than if I'd been given a fine riding crop or a tie pin – after all, it's not such a large house, a few crumbling bricks and a piece of barren land, where even if he strained every sinew, Felipe would never be able to establish a garden worth its salt.

And yet we did laugh – Grandfather told me about his first beautiful gig, a two-wheeled *birlocho*: "In all Madrid," he said, "there were only three like it! Three, my son. In one rode the son of a banker, who came to a bad end later, in another a prince of the blood, and in the third none other than don Francisco de Goya! It was gilded and varnished – when I drove by in it, the whole street stopped, every fishmonger, every orange girl, every matron and street urchin stared after that gewgaw. But the joy only lasted about half an hour: the seller took me for the first ride so I'd be sure everything worked as it should, that the axles were well balanced, and the whole thing didn't sway... but when I whipped the horse and raced down the middle of the road, we all came crashing down in one spot together: the *birlocho*, the horse and I. All I had to show for it was a pile of broken wood, gilded and varnished, and a wounded hand, which I spent two weeks licking better. As I work with my hands, I thought to myself, I must care for them like a violinist. And from then on I drove nothing but quiet mules."

As I listened to him in amusement, right in the middle of his account I realized that the incident itself had been no fun for him at all, he was simply retelling for the umpteenth time a story which he had told to various people over and over. And that the laughter was in the story, not in him. He was nothing but a pair of lips, moving in sorrow.

XVII

Instigations

Grey beard to the waist, hunched shoulders, but Evil is whispering in his ear: put on a pilgrim's cloak, take a cane in your twisted hands and on the road, on the road you go! He cannot hear a thing, not the rain, nor a shout, nor the hooting of an owl, but as if out of spite, he can hear those whispered instigations.

It wasn't meant to be like this: old age was meant to bring wisdom, not delusions. It was meant to be the evening, when you open your eyes from half-sleep and see the truth in all its force and painfulness, having cast off foolish illusions and juvenile hopes. Meanwhile it brings as much deception as youth, or maybe even more, for youth still has some chances of achieving something. Old age only strives towards the damp earth in the depths of the grave.

Like in that drawing: dragging his feet, rheumy-eyed, hair a tangle, a monk in the order of industry, is saying to himself: "Still I learn". But he isn't learning at all. He is being taught by a devil incarnate, who night after night drips little words of hemlock into his ear.

He tries to distinguish wisdom from inanity and the hard essence of things from apparitions woven out of spectral yarn by satanic spinners – there's no help from anywhere. Every indicator, every instigator can lead him astray. So he stretches out his cane and walks ahead, blindly.

XVIII

Francisco:

Now, by the hearth in Bordeaux – with Leocadia at the far end
of the drawing room, laughing as she sets a carafe down on the
side table, orange in the warm glow coming from the fire, with
friends, old and new, with Moratín, with Brugada, who keep
on visiting us – the last few months seem like apparitions,
phantoms of the sleeping mind. And yet: I, Francisco Goya,
an old man of almost eighty, have skipped across the border
like a lark, by post coach! I knew: though the mills of God
grind slowly, yet they'll grab you by the arse eventually and
pulverize you; maybe the inquisitors have forgiven me for the
time being, but just watch them come back. And there will
be no mercy. I transferred the House of the Deaf Man to my
little boy, Mariano, for a couple of months I holed up at the
Buen Suceso hospital, with Father José Duaso – for whomever
they might hurt, no one will touch a Jesuit, the royal chaplain
– and perfectly casually I asked His Supreme Majesty for
permission to travel to the thermal waters at Plombières,
because of this hand, and this foot, it's the dropsy... and as
the king had just announced an amnesty to be rid of all the
liberals, and suddenly the official chambers were starting to
grant permission to leave the kingdom, as if throwing sweets
into the crowd, in the blink of an eye I crossed the Pyrenees.
Afterwards, of course, no soaking my behind at the thermal

springs: first I went to Paris. Marianito has to go there without fail – it is the place for a fashionable young gentleman. What fine riding boots, what fine firearms at the gunsmith's – toys made by master craftsmen! My old French lessons were of no use at all – no one here can understand me, I must have been taught by a blockhead, for I remember almost nothing; but there is someone to talk Spanish to – sometimes I reckon there are more Spaniards here than Frenchmen – lawyers, bankers, painters... I met with the poor Countess Chinchón, whom Godoy is still betraying with Pepita Tudo. A quarter of a century on! Evidently, some things in this world never change. The Sausage-Maker himself has been gadding about all over Europe and can be met in the Tulleries or Tullieres, basking in the sunshine and staring at the children playing games... apparently he is scribbling his memoirs – but who would want to read about how he became a duke, when the only service he ever rendered was to stuff a big sausage under the withered skirts of the old queen? Everyone was urging me to go and see the picture of a shipwreck painted by a young lad, who had in fact died shortly before my arrival, but they say it is large and dark, so I wouldn't have seen anything in any case, even if I put one pair of spectacles on top of the other. Moreover, that wasn't how to paint a shipwreck! Whereas I did see the work of Monsieur Martin, an unrivalled miniaturist: what sweet little things they are. He has been deaf and dumb from birth, which makes him four times more damaged than I, who am merely deaf, and that for only half my life; as I placed those very fine pieces of ivory right under my nose I thought: hey, Paco, if you were four times as handicapped, wouldn't you be afraid of a large canvas? He noticed my checked cap – in Paris it was generally greatly admired, though I don't know why. It's a cap like any other.

None of this is worth mentioning – what counts is here and now, the moment when I saw Leocadia for the first time after so many months, her untamed locks, which only one woman in the world ever had before her! And little Ladybird, and the house in Bordeaux, peace after those months of uncertainty; on the border I thought I would soil my breeches, I could see myself in a vast court room, with my hands manacled, and a *coroza* – a dunce's cap on my head, all my sins painted on it, even the most secret ones... And now? If it goes well, I will live to ninety-nine, like Titian – I wonder if I'll manage to beat him?

Javier:

I couldn't decide whether to keep him here or bundle him off as far away as possible – ten times I wanted to inform the police that he was hiding at Father Duaso's house, that he was planning to escape to France, though he was still in the king's service, and that he had a mistress whose son, sure to be a bastard too, had served in the rebel guards – and ten times I went back home. Well, all right, maybe more like twice.

You will be entirely alone, I thought to myself. With your wife, with Mariano, but on your own, entirely alone, because you'll finally be rid of that burden, that donkey, whom I must carry about on my shoulders, bent double day after day, night after night. I went to bed with a sense of imminent freedom, but at dawn I awoke, sticky with sweat, for in my dream I had seen four brigands or soldiers robbing the coach and murdering all the passengers. In every dream he died a different way, but just as terribly.

Until one day he told me himself that he had finally been given permission, and any moment he was leaving. "Very good," I said, "everyone could do with a bit of rest."

XIX

Leocadia

One conceals the other – like in Godoy's secret study, where the clothed *maja* disappeared, taken off into the darkness by a system of cogs and gears, revealing the naked *maja*, Pepita Tudo, with her belly like a plum, bisected by a long dimple, and her bust wall-eyed, as if each breast were about to slip beneath an armpit – but here there is no machinery, the two pictures are merged together, so tightly conjoined that nothing will ever separate them.

The first one is invisible: she stands, leaning against a marble fireplace, amused, winding a lock of hair around her finger. Has she perhaps been dancing with one of the guests, and now, after hurriedly wiping the pearls of perspiration from her chest with a batiste scarf and letting her shawl slip from her shoulders, is resting, waiting for the blush to leave her burning cheeks? Is she watching as the maid serves sorbets and wondering what prospects she has for an affair with the lithe dancer who so heroically wears the yellow ribbon of the liberals on his arm? Or maybe she is listening to her daughter playing the piano, and raising her brow in amazement that something which came out of her not so long ago, slimy and screaming, is now using her nimble fingers to pick out a series of notes, one by one? She is the mistress of life. She has it all: full keep, peace from her husband, charming children, an undemanding lover and so many men willing to leap into bed with her, as many as she desires.

The second has covered her face with a mourning mantilla – a widow who has no right to be a widow – and that same elbow, which was leaning against the fireplace in the parlour of the apartment in Bordeaux, is now touching the cold, damp earth, in which a grave has been dug; if she stretched out her arm, she would touch the iron fence which encloses the still fresh mound. That is not a blush, it is just that the face has gone red from weeping. It is not desires that are raising her brow, but disappointment. "So that's it already? So soon?"

If you believe the saying that the truth is naked – although it is nonsense, for even nakedness is a lie – then the true *maja* has hidden behind the false, clothed *maja*; here it is the truth that covers the lie, for it is despair that is the hard stone of the world, all that will be left of a fruit that rots in the sun.

XX

Francisco:

Here in Bordeaux my dreams are completely different; my life is coming back to me in its full variety; in my dreams I feel as if I'm living outside time. I have three small children, Javier, Mariano and Rosario, and the perfect wife, who is half Pepa, and half Leocadia. I dreamed of Javier's old painting, the broad back of the giant. Armies went rolling across the fields, it was desolate: he was sitting on the borders of the world, under a starry sky and watching, his face turned towards me, as if asking about something or waiting for a confession.

Javier:

Ever since he left, I have more dreams, and at dawn I can remember the dreams like long stories, as if I no longer had to read, as if the stories were creating themselves, proliferating all on their own; some images evolve into others and engender more, as if constantly on heat. I could sleep for days on end – but not as I once did, so as not to feel or see anything, but on the contrary – so as to feel and see as much as possible.

Francisco:

There's so much going on here! Sometimes I doze off in the

middle of the day, and as soon as I awake I regret having slept through as little as half an hour: sometimes I feel as if I have gone back to childhood, when every hour brings something new. If I am not painting with my little Ladybird or drawing bulls on stone... ah, how much a man remembers in spite of all! Pepe Illo, nailed to the arena by a pair of horns, I saw that with my own eyes... Pedro Romero, a dear friend, with whom many a... eh, never mind about that. And La Pajuelera? How could I forget her! La Paluejera, all those years ago in Zaragoza – the great Escamilla, who stuck in the sword with just the same charm as in the past, when she still walked the streets, selling trinkets and handing out boxes of matches...

The French may not have the *corrida*, but right next to our house there is a small theatre, where they show the most wonderful little plays; a week ago we had the Mouse Devourer – what a pity I didn't sketch him: he bit off their heads, drank their blood and hurled the remains to the sand or into the crowd – and yesterday there was the Incombustible Arab, who came, as I did, straight from Paris: he jumped into an oven whole, and then, like in those biblical tales, came out of there unharmed, clutching a nicely browned chicken, to which he then treated the audience... Leocadia got a piece of wing and said she couldn't have roasted it better herself.

I love to look at her when we go to the theatre or a circus show; it is she whom I go there to watch, and not the Living Skeleton, in other words the walking bones draped in skin, not the snakes and crocodiles, nor Hercules the tightrope walker. It is enough for me that her full round face, ever more lovely, is flushed at the circus, that her cheeks are suffused with restless, warm blood – everything that she sees, I see reflected, in her face. I watch the movement of her eyes, the tiny twitches at the corners of her lips, and it is as if I were seeing in full splendour

Satan on Horseback Defeated by the Exterminating Angel or the winged stunt rider Avillon, jumping on the trapeze with Madame Rosalie... And how much joy we had with Munito! Ah, in my life I have had the most splendid hunting dogs, unrivalled at fetching in the game, but I must admit that none of them was capable of the same acts as Munito, who could count, play dominoes, write out letters and distinguish colours. Rosario's favourite performances were by Monsieur... Monsieur... what was his name? Never mind that: le Pétomane, who could play entire tunes on his rear and imitate all sorts of animals too. I could hear nothing, of course, but how we laughed, it was such fun! Then we went to Poc's for chocolate, on the Rue de la Petite-Taupe. Every time little Rosario is pleased we are going to "the little mole's street", less perhaps by the chocolate, and more by the name, but I'm not going to explain to her that their little moles are our *lechuzas* – "little owls", in other words cheap whores. To each country its own customs, to each country its own little beasties.

They also have boots on wheels here, very fashionable among the young people – you can see them riding down the avenues in the parks and along the streets, tumbling over now and then. The public also goes to executions, I have seen two, but for me it is nothing new: I have seen more than enough people being deprived of their lives, and I don't find the French method a jot better or more merciful than the Spanish.

I wrote to Javier to say they must be sure to come and see us here – the longer a man lives, the more he appreciates the joy of spending time with his family. Whatever it may be like. But there's no reply, silence. His excuse is a lack of time – ha, he could just as well not bother writing to tell me that, but fart it out instead like the flatulist from the circus. Even then I wouldn't believe him.

Javier:

I refused to travel to Bordeaux for so long that he came here himself, curse him. Apparently he was so unwell in the spring that he gained permission for further treatment at the waters. Probably not at the waters, but at the springs of Bordeaux, if I know him. First he sent a letter drafted by two doctors saying that he was suffering from sclerosis of the bowels, a tumour in the groin and paralysis of the bladder, and that he absolutely could not travel; I had to take it to the royal office and hand it in with a straight face, in a perfectly casual way. But as soon as he got a year's extension of leave, as if all twelve apostles had worked a miracle he recovered, and descended upon us. He said he had to make sure he was awarded a retirement pension from the royal coffers, but I now know that he only came so he could stick his nose into other people's affairs, do a bit of swaggering, and have his fill – not so much of Madrid, but of himself in Madrid – to blow his own trumpet and strike poses. He talked nothing but sheer nonsense: about the Skeleton Man, about a giantess displayed at the fair, perfectly proportioned, but two heads taller than the average man, and about some suspicious characters at a chocolate shop who don't have proper names, just nicknames: the Shepherd, the Doctor, Waistcoat... And Mariano and Gumersinda listened to him as if bewitched, as if it meant something. Of course he also had to scrawl Mariano's portrait, though he can hardly see a thing – when the king sent the court painter, López, to paint a portrait of "the famous Goya", he threatened to paint López at once in return. But he has arthritic fingers and a blind eye. I even had to find the brushes and palette for him. And when the time came, he painted Marianito at a single sitting, the old fox.

Mariano:

It was hard to talk to my grandfather about the most important things – not because he had nothing to say about them, on the contrary, but because the most important things need a lot of words.

My father has never understood anything that is sublime; my grandfather told me – first asking if I can keep a secret – that there is a scientific explanation for this, which he heard from a man who studied chemistry: it is lead white, the fine dust from sanded canvases which always coated everything in the studio. It poisons the body, very slowly, but thoroughly. But in his opinion the paints have nothing to do with it, that is just the delusions of doctors, and you can't expect anything good from doctors. "He has always been like that," he said, "like a dummy, tossed in a blanket by a bunch of women, with no will of his own. As if he'd had everything cut off higher up, you understand, upstairs. He eats, shits, and even produced you, though probably without any special desire, just for the sake of propriety, but when he has to reach for something of a higher order, something intangible, nothing remains in his hand. That is how he was born."

Francisco:

In Bordeaux I saw a madhouse, I drew there until it went dark: lunatics sobbing on their knees, roaring and furiously thrashing about in their cells, poking their heads through the bars. In their infinite innocence they reminded me of two other lunatics, from years ago – but I must be quiet about this. If anyone were to ask me, I would prefer to sit there with them and listen to their screams than talk about nothing in Javier's parlour; I can't bear holding a conversation with that empty shell, in which there is nothing left alive.

And yet, as soon as I went back to France, I missed them all; whenever I dozed off – it happens to me more and more often – I could see them as clearly as if they were sitting opposite me. I send off letter after letter – every time there are some excuses. Even though I write plainly that I will cover all the costs of the journey, they won't have to spend a single *real* on it.

At other times I tell myself: you impatient old codger, what's your hurry? You still have years to go to reach Titian's age!

Javier:

All my life I have read a lot, that may be the only thing I have ever been any good at, and I know how to read between the words as well as I can read the words themselves. I knew the end was approaching, which Doctor Arrieta predicted many years ago: well, the day of reckoning has come for the old goat.

Here's another *Caprice*: on a bed we see the profile of a dying old man in a nightcap, and under the bed – a black figure against the white sheets – his young lover is rifling through his chests. He could let himself be taken in, but I am not. France sent One Hundred Thousand Sons of Saint Louis to our rescue, and I sent Gumersinda to France with the lad, to rescue our property. So now we're quits.

XXI

Mariano:

My mother complained throughout the journey, under her breath. About the passengers, about the coachman, about the potholes. Under her breath, in a whisper, bzz-bzz-bzz. On and on, day after day. She only stopped when she went to bed, but even then I could hear her muttering in her sleep behind the partition. Bzz-bzz-bzz. We arrived late in the afternoon on the twenty-eighth, to be in time for the birthday. His eighty-second. Typically for my grandfather, he got more pleasure from seeing us than from the presents we brought. And he was more pleased with what he had prepared for us than with what he received from us. What he was going to receive, for he didn't get that far. On arrival the first day we found Brugada and Molina, whom Grandfather had been painting recently; the unfinished painting is still standing on the easel, covered by a thin cloth. We listened to Rosario playing some jolly pieces on the piano which she had just learned – and it was nice that Grandfather, who had been wanting to drag Molina into the studio "for just ten little minutes" to finish the portrait, or at least to add a new layer of shade and work on the coat a little, had decided instead to stay and "listen to Rosario", although of course he couldn't hear a single note; he was happy to watch her running her fingers over the keyboard and sticking out her tongue at the harder passages; he had more fun doing that than he would from watching the greatest *toreros* of his youth.

On the twenty-ninth we ate an early dinner together, with doña Leocadia and little Rosario, wearing her best dress, all at the same table, which cost Mama a few nerves; the only one missing was Guillermo, who had left the city for two days. After dinner I helped Grandfather to move into the parlour, but he said that thanks to our arrival he had regained such a strong appetite that he had overeaten horribly, or to be more precise: "stuffed my guts", and had to lie down.

Next day, on Grandfather's birthday, I was awoken by shouts – it was doña Leocadia, who rushed into the room looking all dishevelled, her face red from weeping and fretting, and began to explain incoherently that he had awoken at five in the morning and couldn't say a word; he had dragged himself out of bed, then fallen as if struck by a thunderbolt, with half his body completely paralysed; she had called the maid and with her help had hauled him back to bed, and sent for the doctor.

Of course nothing came of the birthday; the cook was told to do something with the food so that not everything prepared for the festive dinner would be spoiled, so when everyone had sunk into reverie, then began talking to each other again nervously, in rapid, incomplete sentences, from the kitchen came the odour of the marinade and the steady tapping of the chopper against the board, with occasional cries of "Pour it in, off you go!" at which my mother just rolled her eyes and hissed "Lord have mercy!" I shut myself in my room and stared vacantly at the last present from my grandfather: a beautiful gilded penknife made of English steel which he had brought specially for me from Paris. I still have it to this day.

After a few hours he regained his voice, but he was very feeble. Two weeks of death agony began. My mother set up watch by his bed and was extraordinary about it; at his beck and call, responsive to every breath, hardly sleeping two hours in every twenty-four, and bearing the discomfort with stoical dignity, just as if a few days earlier she hadn't been complaining about every single flea, scratch or bump all the way from Madrid to Bordeaux, a true allegory of care, in the style of Mengs; only towards the end did I understand what she meant by it. She did her best not to let anyone into the bedroom; a rumour had already gone around about a serious malady and people kept coming by to bid farewell to "the master"; she sent them away with a flea in their ear. She made an exception for doña Leocadia – just as if she herself were the mistress here, and not a guest – but that too with the utmost, totally undisguised reluctance. And also for his old friends, Molina and Brugada, who isn't actually at all old, as he is only two years my senior. Even when the cook, just like that, of her own will, unasked, out of the goodness of her heart tried to bring my grandfather some water, Mama came out of the room, shut the door behind her, took the glass and only went back inside once the cook had waddled downstairs. And even then she opened the door such a narrow crack that nothing could be seen through it, just the left half of a large wardrobe. And throughout the process she didn't say a word.

He hardly said a thing either; at moments he gibbered indistinctly, though sometimes you could understand a phrase or two; when his breathing weakened, Brugada supported his head for him, as long as he was on the spot at the time. It looked as if he would have been happy to be there for the duration, but my mother made it clear to him that she did not wish him to stay. Not straight out, but simply by not answering his questions, showing impatience, and pursing her lips. Rosario was not allowed to cross the threshold at all, because this was "not the place for children"; my mother wanted to try the same thing with me, but she was a few years too late; and so I did drop in on Grandfather whenever I came back from town, for in the end how much time can you spend cooped up in the house of a sick man, where from dawn to dusk you must walk about on tiptoes and talk in a whisper, with a pained look on your face perforce; for two nights or so, I admit, I was out on the town, but I don't think Grandfather would have had any objection to that – I was there however the evening when he regained the use of his hand, and now and then it was possible to understand what he was saying; I was standing next to my mother just as she was putting a cold compress to his brow, and at that moment I clearly heard: "I want to make a bequest for Leocadia and Rosario", but in the same soothing voice in which she had been addressing him since the first day of the illness, the voice of an angel, the slick, Mengs-style allegory of care, my mother said: "You've already made a bequest, Papa, hush now, hush, shhhh..."; he opened his eyes, and stared at her blankly, in surprise, as if he couldn't believe he was mistaken, and she repeated: "Yes, everything's fine, there now..." Only then did he close his eyes and sink into light, fitful sleep. "You're lucky doña Leocadia wasn't here just then, Mama," I muttered, and she shot me a look, glaring in anger, then turned to face the bed.

When he died, I wasn't at home; I was on my way back from town, never mind where I'd been. It was just after two, and as soon as I reached the doorstep I could tell it was all over – there was something in the air. Doña Leocadia – how odd that it was her, now that I think about it – was the first to come up to me, sniffling, and say: "He died as if he'd fallen asleep... even the doctor... was surprised how much... how much strength he had in him... they say he didn't suffer" – at this point her voice faltered – "but it's not true... it's not true." And she walked off, in such a strange way, tripping on a completely smooth floor.

XXII

Javier:

The letter came in the first week of April, perhaps at the very start of the second week – but I could sense he was still alive. Strange days. I walked about Madrid in anticipation of the tremendous freedom that was approaching me, flying in on mighty wings from the Pyrenees – just as the *afrancesados* once waited for Napoleon and his Constitution, and later how the mob waited for El Deseado, the longed-for king returning from exile, before he turned out to be a cretin and a despot, and how even later on his dwindling supporters waited for the One Hundred Thousand Sons of Saint Louis (can you imagine a more idiotic name for those thieving French soldiers?), so I too, as I went for my stroll, turned to face the Pyrenees – well, roughly, let's say – hoping to feel a breath of wind on my cheeks that would bring me a foretaste of freedom. In the meantime I saw to various essential matters: a copy of my birth certificate, which I had authenticated by the royal notary, and the permission of the French consul general. I did not even take the carriage, I preferred to stroll; it was spring, everything was sticky, pulsating with sap, and in the forty-third year of my life I was being born for the second time. To what end – how was I to know? Who can know on the day of his birth to what end he is being born?

And then I sensed, all of a sudden, that he had died.

And that I wouldn't find him alive when I got there, that I wouldn't have to look him in the eyes and put up with that disdainful expression, those embittered grudges and musty old resentments. Finally I could make the journey. I knew Gumersinda was on the spot, keeping an eye on our affairs and Marianito's. As soon as he died a crowd of people came rolling through the house. Gaulon, the man in the lithograph, who later helped me with the will, summoned someone called de la Torre to draw the old badger on his deathbed; I saw it, nothing special, but they're sure to earn a bit on the prints. Some merchant whom he once painted paid for the funeral, Molina registered his demise at the mayor's office – he got the age wrong, but never mind. Gumersinda buried the old man beside her father, at the Chartreuse cemetery; ultimately, why not? I don't think they'd have fallen out with each other. She took care of all the rest, received the Spanish consul, who had to see the corpse and confirm the identity, bought a habit from the Franciscans, because the old man wanted to be buried in a monk's habit, and also paid extra for mourners, which she could just as well have done without, and finally reassured that woman that as soon as I arrived, everything would be settled and we would divide the estate fairly.

And divide it we did. First of all I looked for the pistols, because I knew for sure that they were very valuable and of the best quality; when it came to any kind of tool for killing, slashing, opening veins or smashing skulls, my father always had good taste and never spared the money. Then I saw to the silver, which speaks for itself; luckily the servants had taken proper care of that, at least, and to the day of my arrival nothing had been lost; just one small plate had gone astray. But someone remembered that it was lying by the bed in which the old man had died. I went upstairs – it had already been neatly remade, and there in the middle lay a small, wilted bouquet, brought in by Rosario, most likely. I picked up the plate and stood there for a while. I thought about him – how he couldn't stand sentimental gestures, and never painted flowers. If she wanted to please him, she should have put a guinea fowl with a twisted neck on the bed, or a skinned calf's head, something he could have painted – but how could such a prim-and-proper, silly little girl with her neat, boring pencil strokes understand that? Flowers, flowers. Ugh. I took the plate, went into the kitchen and made sure everything was packed up properly and sent to Madrid.

And then I went to that woman and told her, dryly and rather forcefully, as I had no intention of making a scene or savouring her downfall; I had no intention of admitting that it was any sort of triumph for me; so I told her like this, dryly and forcefully, and yet quite magnanimously, as I see it: "You are in a foreign country and perhaps you would like to return to your own; here is a banker's draft for a thousand francs – that should be enough." I wanted to add something to the effect that her husband must surely be greatly looking forward to her return, but that would have been mean. "You can keep the furniture and the clothing," was all I added. She started to tell some story about how she was already looking for cheaper accommodation, but that Francisco was meant to have made provision for her in his will, that there were some bequests, and apart from that there was the piano, she would have to sell the piano, which would be an awful blow for Rosario – that was how she spoke, higgledy-piggledy, getting tangled in several threads at once, so there I stood, for what was I to do? holding a scrap of paper worth a thousand francs between finger and thumb; finally I stuffed it into her hand and said: "If there are any bequests for you, please find them and be sure to take them to the notary. But now, please excuse me, I have matters to attend to." I bowed, but not excessively, merely raising a hand to the brim of my hat, and left the room. The rent was paid to the end of the month, we all had to get out of that house, so I went to find a decent hotel, where Gumersinda, Marianito and I could stay.

XXIII

The Dog

The dog is alone. Entirely alone. A lonely dog is an unfortunate dog. Some people think it is drowning in quicksand, others that it is merely poking its head out from behind a sun-baked hill; but the dog doesn't care if it is drowning or running across never-ending, scorched earth, across boiling hot ash. Because it doesn't care about anything.

Even if one were to calculate the surface area of the dog's head: a floppy ear, a patch of neck, the black dot of a snuffling nose and the white of a hankering eye, and if one were to see how many times it would fit into the vast expanse that lies fallow, van Dyck's dirty brown, ochre whitened by the burning light (and a touch of lead white), even if one were to divide this great void by the lack of a void, in other words the solitary dog's head, it is impossible to comprehend how greatly it is suffering.

The world and its variety; the smells – those trailing close to the ground and those carried on the wind. The smell of a leather strap, the pungent odour of gunpowder and the thin trail – that's a shot-down duck, falling from on high and landing in the sparse undergrowth with a dry crack; whole registers of aromas coming from the city: gutters, perfumed necks, heads of cabbage starting to rot in the sun on market stalls, ripe melons all but bursting with juice; the blood at the slaughterhouse, sickening, savage, flowing in a broad stream to the stone runnel and on, into the street; and everything that's close by: a mole, sun-baked herbs, the master's boots as he raises his flintlock again and aims it at another duck; the world and its variety – and yet without him, it seems entirely devoid of expression, as unexciting as a flat wall. The nostrils – which could draw a complete map of the vicinity, with fixed points (the pissed-on wall of an inn, the gateway into a church exuding incense, the tannery by the stream) and moving ones (dogs, cats, cows driven along a white-hot road, people and their variety of smells) – are now helpless; some say despair can take away the senses – if it can take them away from people, why wouldn't it take them from a dog?

First of all, it missed the good things: a warm bed by the fireplace, scraps of meat, rare caresses when its master had nothing to do, and rubbed or scratched its back on a whim; then it missed the ordinary things: running about the farmyard, about the neighbourhood, sharing his presence. Now it even misses the stick and the chain to which it was sometimes shackled as a punishment. It misses the stick falling on its back, and the shrill squeal that emerged from its throat, because at the other end of the stick there was a clenched hand, the hand of its master.

XXIV

Javier:

I don't know what I imagined. Then, in Madrid, when I was trying to feel a breeze from the Pyrenees on my face. What did I think it would bring? I thought freedom was Freedom, an earthquake that would uplift valleys and reduce mountains to dust, and that where it appeared, nothing would be the same as before – yet meanwhile we came home from Bordeaux, took care of the paperwork, executed the will, paid out money to all the spongers to whom my father, at my mother's request, had left a few *reales* each – hospitals, pilgrims' homes in Jerusalem, and so on; somehow we dealt with Leocadia and her claims... and suddenly it turned out a year had gone by, an entire year, and I wasn't the least bit freer than in the past.

Of course, I had more money – but was I poor before then? With a father like that? Business was going well, and if it went worse for a while, there was always a whole heap of paintings to sell. A genuine Goya from the most reliable source. And for a rainy day there were the pictures I got from the division of my mother's will before he ran away from Spain: Coreggio, Velázquez, Rembrandt prints, you name it. And he might have given up in his old age, but no, he went on pulling his cart like a mule, like a heavy horse, doing this, doing that, both engravings, and portraits, and drawings, and miniatures; he was blind as a bat, deaf as a post, and weak as a jellyfish, and still he went on sitting there tinkering, painting and erasing, and painting again, as if whatever was churning around in that bunged-up old pate of his could only find an outlet through his fingers, onto paper, onto lithographic stone, onto a sliver of ivory, onto a page in a sketchpad; and how it excited him, how badly he wanted to look, to feed those half-blind eyes of his on the sight of everything – vagrants, roller-skaters, madmen. Even in Bordeaux, with three pairs of spectacles, hardly able to walk, he had himself taken to a lunatic asylum and spent the whole day there, drawing incessantly, until there wasn't enough light. And when there was nothing interesting to look at, he slept. He even worked in his sleep, fantasizing, and then he offloaded those fantasies onto paper. That man was a factory producing *escudos*, *reales* and doubloons, he was like a miniature mint with an endless supply of ore. For as long as I can remember there were never any problems with money – perhaps during the war, when the king was exiled and no one was paying him a salary; but even then he painted King Pepe Botella's adjutant, some French general, whatever he was called... and that ghastly *Allegory of Madrid*, of which he said that the allegorical figure had an... pardon the expression, an I-won't-say-what of marble, and that afterwards they redid it over and over again, every time someone else captured the city... and later on he painted Wellington, on his horse, oh dear, on that very unsuccessful horse, oh dear, very unsuccessful indeed. And how he raged as he did that horse – he even threw a glass at the maid! Well, he was never any good at horses.

I thought I would be free, but he was still hanging over me, a great big corpse, as if preserved in alcohol – he was rotting somewhere far away, in the Chartreuse cemetery, next to my even more thoroughly decomposed father-in-law, but he was still hanging over me, whole, intact, just as he was in life. With his eyes open, and that same look of disdain and disappointment in them. Perhaps it's because I didn't see him dead? Perhaps I should have gone there earlier and watched him exhale his last, wheezy, whistling breath? Maybe then I'd have had peace? Or if I'd seen them with my own eyes, sewing up his dead body in a Franciscan habit, ripped up the back, as they are for the deceased, and placing him in his coffin, or if I'd seen the wet spring earth, rich with life, thudding against the lid?

And it was only a good year after his death, one day, when we had driven out of town, to the Quinta del Sordo, and Gumersinda and I were eating in the room upstairs... no, just a moment, no, there wasn't an upstairs yet then. We were on the ground floor. We had them set out the table downstairs, and serve the food we had brought from Madrid, and the things we had got from the farmhand; a simple, country meal: some cold chicken, olives, gazpacho... yes, it must have been chicken, because I remember that it occurred to me... yes, I remember that moment precisely: I was chewing on a wing, gazing at Gumersinda, no, not even at her, at a piece of the wall just behind her, a piece of the wall papered in yellow calico with a tiny golden pattern, and she raised a glass to her lips... and at that very moment it occurred to me that the same thing was meant to happen when the old man left for Bordeaux: we were already rid of Leocadia, who had gone first, to find them a nest and feather it properly, line it with nice little silks and cushions, all niminy-piminy, as if he gave a damn, and at once life had become pleasanter, calmer, it was even possible to talk to him more normally somehow, or at least to listen to him mumbling about paintings, and to watch him drawing a line on a copper plate with a thin engraving tool; he had already managed to transfer the Quinta del Sordo to Marianito, it was all just for the time being. Even his presence, which had always flooded every house he ever lived in, saturated every coat of dust in the corner, every ball of hair in the upholstery of an armchair, was weaker, like dimmed light. And I remembered that then too I had felt a sense of approaching freedom, as if the dams and sluices were opening, which held back a great, seething river flowing inside me, for all these years hidden underground, walled in. He went away, and nothing happened.

But Mariano's wedding had to be organized, and I forgot about it all.

Mariano:

We were united – can I say that? – we were united by a love of music. And of... well, quite – of a beautiful life. For we were both – after all, we're not going to hide it, because it's impossible to hide – beautiful. And our surroundings were beautiful too; for compared with everything there was to dislike about Spain, that squalid province of Paris, we had lots of splendour all around us; we were both rich, and it looked as if we could only grow richer from year to year; Concepción was getting a dowry from her father of a kind that might be envied by many a far less good-looking young lady whose father was keen to hustle her out of his "good home" at almost any price; Fatso gave me something, not much perhaps, at any rate less than he could have, but I did have capital put aside by my grandfather – it is touching how hard he worked, to the very end of his days, to make it up to a round sum of twelve thousand as the annual dividend. A good thousand a month. Not that he denied himself anything in particular: he lived comfortably, he rented a perfectly nice little house, where he lived with that mistress of his, he always had his fill of chocolate with milk and cinnamon, so I had no pangs of conscience. Anyway, isn't it the duty of the old to secure the future of their offspring?

And so we were secure, she and I, I and she.

Javier:

I would have preferred Madrid, but Mariano insisted on having the wedding party at the House of the Deaf Man. Not in that old ruin that remembered the shrieks of a certain lady and an old badger, wiping his fat, paint-soiled fingers on the floor and scrawling caricatures of people he knew on the walls, but in a new house, furnished to suit a sophisticated young master. What had to suffice for my father became nothing but a shameful hinterland with a lumber room, rooms for the servants and a kitchen. Alongside there rose an entirely new building, separated from the old one by large gates into an atrium, which reached almost to the roof of the first floor; downstairs and upstairs there was one large room and a couple of very small ones; below there was a drawing room, and above a large study, which was to become a music room, and the double staircase was like in a giants' palace, splendid, with a bust of the famous Goya on the landing – I'm sorry, "de Goya" – on a pedestal; in short, it was like the Escorial.

Carpenters, painters and plasterers went running up and down for days on end; we hacked off every last line of what the old man had scribbled during his jolly booze-ups: Doctor Arrieta in a mantilla, pretending to be a respectable matron, old Weiss with his paws on a bag of gold, drooling over the coins, Felipe with a leaky watering can, ladies of the night brought along by some man or other, and with whom apparently that woman at once found a common language, which doesn't surprise me in the least. I tried to find a way of preserving it all somehow, by sticking the bits of plaster onto canvas, but they fell to pieces, so I dropped the idea – anyway, who would want to buy and hang on the wall caricatures of strangers and uninteresting people? Of me, for instance: a fat, shapeless lump squeezed into a frock coat, dripping tears into a cup of herbal tea. No one, I reckon – it's no loss.

The building work ordered by Mariano seemed to me incoherent and absurd: for how can you combine a monumental staircase and a tumbledown cottage? So did his plans to convert the garden into an English park, with flowerbeds going to seed, tended by Felipe with one little hoe. You only had to walk through two doors, and from the marble stairs you came to a shabby little larder. The bust was supposed to be made of pink marble, but for now it was waiting to be carved; it was made of plaster and painted to look like a piece of stone. "Who will spot the difference?" asked Mariano, "and on a wedding day, when they're half cut? Well, perhaps someone'll be drunk enough to lean against the pedestal and knock the head down the stairs. But I hope it doesn't come to that!" We brought out the best paintings from Madrid – the House of the Deaf Man was to be a great mausoleum, a celebrity morgue, a catafalque, on which Mariano would enter the bonds of holy matrimony, drawing strength from his grandfather's remains, decomposing in a graveyard in Bordeaux. Yum-yum.

Mariano:

Enough scrimping and saving, enough griping that everything's so expensive, that we'll have to break into the next thousand of the annual allowance, that cheaper is better than costlier. Someone in this family must start to live life to the full. If no one is interested, I can offer myself as a volunteer.

Madrid is a hole, but we brought out all the best things we could, from candelabras and furniture to musical instruments. Uncle Goicoechea gave us a beautiful mahogany table with stands for notes, and Concepción's aunt gave us a porcelain dinner service of the best quality. If my grandfather was a rough diamond unearthed from the dirty soil of Fuendetodos, I will be a cut and polished gem.

XXV

Javier:

In those days I hardly ever spoke to Gumersinda any more – like a typical married couple. We never went back to things from the past, the most ancient matters, nor to more recent ones either: my father's protracted death and my late arrival. In spite of all her shortcomings, of which there are certainly quite a few, my wife has always had a sort of subtlety about her, or perhaps to put it better, an intuition that told her to keep quiet about certain matters more than all the rest. Once, I recall, Mariano told me that his mother was one of those talkative types, and I was greatly surprised to hear him say it – indeed, she spoke to other people more often, but in my company she generally said nothing. I don't know, perhaps she simply didn't like me – in fact I didn't really know her well enough to be able to judge; each of us tried to fulfil his marital obligations as far as he was capable. Can one demand any more of a person?

And yet there were times, even in later years, when we quarrelled – to this day I do not understand how it is possible for two people, who do in fact live under the same roof, but in a capacious enough house for them to avoid each other all day long, so they never once look each other in the eye, nevertheless to tend towards unnecessary outbursts of emotion. All the more since with time all the words uttered with such bitterness, all the causes for complaint disappear, disintegrate and sink into oblivion; there is nothing left of the quarrelling, absolutely nothing, not counting a little bit of silt, a stinking sediment which accumulates in the crannies of the so-called soul. And of all the quarrels, the one that has remained deepest within me, that has eaten into the tissue of my memory, involves that scene I refused to attend – my father's last words. For years she spared me that, she said nothing that could have put me onto the right track, but one day she did not hold back – and the funniest thing is that we weren't arguing about anything important... aren't the most painful quarrels always about the most trivial matters? Isn't it the trifles – a knocked-over glass, a stain on a coat, being late for supper – that make us react with the meanest insults, and inflict the most painful blows? So indeed it was about something trivial, a torn-off button, failing to send a thank-you letter – and suddenly from two civilized, gradually ageing people we changed into crazed mules, biting each other on the highway with teeth as big as spades; and even though we remained separated by a long table, even though neither of us raised a hand to the other, though we were still wearing decently-cut clothing buttoned right up to the neck, we really were those enraged mules, biting to the blood, whinnying with pain and cruel fury, and we hurled the most vile abuse at each other; he who wants to inflict the most painful wound either keeps hitting on the same spot, striking the unhealed bruises, or where we are not expecting any blow to land; and once she had struck in all the places where my father used to hit me, once I had heard that I am a fat layabout, a failure, a pitiful oaf, the laughing stock of the whole city, a capon, a nonentity, the artist who has never painted a single picture, once she had opened all the wounds, each of which unfurled in turn, like large, painful roses, then, as if delivering

157

the final blow with a sword she screamed: "And you don't even know, you clown, what your father's last words were!"

She was right, I didn't. I wasn't there, I hadn't been with them in Bordeaux, at the time I was walking about Madrid, waiting for that tiny pinprick which would tell me: "Now, Javier, it's now. You can go." And she looked at me, her face suddenly so fierce, her lips so tightly clenched as to be white with rage, a blush suffusing her cheeks as if she had spent half the day extracting loaves from the oven, and a thin coil of hair that had come loose and was stuck to her perspiring brow like a little black viper. "I don't know," I said, trying to calm down, in the hope that she would calm down too; but she clenched her lips even tighter – "it's true. I don't know." She went on standing there, silent, purple, like a schoolmaster waiting for the stupidest pupil to answer, purely in order to make fun of him. "Leocadia?" I said hesitantly; she shook her head. "I don't know... Alba?" Not that either. So it was the worst thing possible. "Where's that cringing Javier?"

"No," she spat through her teeth, and then chanted word by word: "Hubby dear, your father's last words were..." No, I can't say them. I won't repeat them.

XXVI

Mariano:

Madrid is what it is, but on the Manzanares it was even worse. Sometimes there was no one to chat to for the entire day except the flies and one old muleteer, slowly driving home to his little wife, who would give him some broth. I tried to do something with the garden, but that good-for-nothing Felipe would rather turn himself inside out than get down to some honest work; he does nothing but grumble that this makes him sore, that makes him sick, his stomach is aching, his nose is itching... If the English lords had gardeners like him, they'd still be living in the wilderness. And if they had cooks like that too they'd be feeding on raw meat and roots.

So much work invested, so many ideas and brainwaves in the middle of the night; a long cascade, some romantic ruins, a broken statue... all for nothing, for nothing, for nothing.

We came there less and less often – mainly to play music with our friends in the music room. We brought food hampers from the city and played, sometimes until first light, then we got in our carriages and were off like greased lightning, back to civilization!

Finally I told Fatso I'd had enough of the old pile, and that either I'd sell it, or if he wanted, I would transfer it back to him – after all, if my grandfather hadn't passed it over to me for fear of it being confiscated, it would have gone to the fat fool with the rest of the estate.

"If you're giving it, I can take it," he said, "yes, I will take it." And that very morning he packed up, stooped to get into his carriage and had himself driven to the Manzanares, not far from the Bridge of Segovia. Who'd have expected it?

XXVII

Javier:

I had thought there was nothing left of him here; we hacked his scrawling off the walls before the wedding, and Felipe burned his old junk in the garden. And yet how long objects can last, how many of them there are! What an unstoppable element – in corners, in lumber rooms, in the attic I was simply wading in the old man's things.

It was strange to pick up all the tools that he hadn't taken away to France with him: brushes with chewed ends and with some of the hairs plucked out, some gone hard for ever, stuck together with paint, others completely bald; scarves, coarse bits of rag, various wooden battens and scrapers he used to groove the surface of the paintings; chipped bowls for mixing colours, spattered with all sorts of stains (flesh pink, indigo, brownish red; cleavages, skies and frock coats from years ago) and little bottles containing the remains of something which perhaps once upon a time was fit for painting, but had long ago gone rancid or mouldy, or dried into a lump. Only the pigments contained the same mineral purity as ever; ground to a fine powder, their unsullied colours radiated from under a layer of dust; they alone, intact paints in a state of complete virginity, were still fit for use. I opened drawer after drawer, and rummaged in their corners (I found a complete set of plates for *Los Disparates*, on which he had been working before

leaving; he hadn't made a single print from them; I wrapped
them up again in thin felt and set them to one side); I moved
aside some unfinished, abandoned paintings – there weren't
many of them, as after giving away his stock of canvas for lint
and bandages for Zaragoza, he only used old stretchers, from
which he scraped off the paint and painted over them again –
in the course of my prospecting I excavated the entire studio.
Without any great success. And only then did I remember the
box that I was given for my fourteenth or fifteenth birthday;
with those paints I had once painted *The Colossus* and a few
tiny little pictures, but then I had abandoned them and buried
them in my room. When we were furnishing the apartments
for Mariano and Concepción, we brought a lot of old junk
out to the country; it had all been tossed in a heap in one of
the unused rooms in the older part of the house, next to some
outmoded rococo wardrobes left by my mother, full of her
moth-eaten dresses and shawls, and the colourful *majo* clothes
my father had worn in his youth, before he went deaf; the door
into the room was locked, so I leaned out of the window and
shouted to Felipe, who was doing some trimming or digging
in the garden. He came, scratched his nose, inspected the
doorknob and the lock, and said: "It was so long ago, how am
I to know where the key to it is, if you please, sir. Better to
buy something new than to look in there." I told him to go to
the shed, bring a crowbar and prise the door open, and then he
started to complain again, that it was a pity to break the lock
and there was no need to make a mess, perhaps the key could
still be found, and went off to the shed to ferret about in places
known only to himself. He finally discovered it in a little bowl
for keys, on a nail banged into the wall, or some other such
place.

Sunlight was falling through the window, drawing jagged

squares on the wall – which in this part of the house was completely raw, not even whitewashed, covered in bumps and splinters. I brought up a chair for myself with a ripped seat, which I found lying about in a corner, wiped it tolerably clean with a handkerchief and sat down on the edge, to avoid dirtying my clothes. It was getting hotter and hotter, but Felipe still hadn't a thought of coming. On and on he searched and rummaged. Finally, complaining of the heat (and what was I supposed to say, condemned to sit in this blazing hot corridor, because he didn't feel like hurrying, not to mention keeping the keys in one place?), he came trailing in from the shed, triumphantly holding a key between finger and thumb. He put it in the lock, then yanked and yanked at it, but with no result. He reached into his pocket and took out about six more keys, having no idea which doors or pieces of furniture they fitted in the house; on the fourth attempt he succeeded, not without difficulty, because the lock hadn't been opened since long ago.

Inside there was a smell of mice and dust baked in the hot air. Felipe stood in the doorway and reluctantly peeped inside, while I, being careful not to twist an ankle on some broken-off chair leg or prised-open box lid (someone must have looked around in here; maybe that was why Felipe was so slow to bring the key?), went deeper and deeper into the forest of redundant things from yesteryear, and became more and more covered in dust, my hands blacker and blacker from digging in the remains of our family life. But I was not mistaken – at the very back of one of the wardrobes from Madrid, under a pile of my mother's shawls, I found my old box of paints; stylish, beautifully lacquered, with once shiny, now rather dull metal fittings, it still looked like a wonderful present for a novice painter; on the lid – I searched about for a bit of rag, and finally wiped it with one of the shawls – I could see two stains; brown toned down with green, which had dripped from my brush while I was painting *The Colossus*, and dove-grey blue, I no longer remembered where from; I started to cough, and coughed without stopping until I put the box down on a nearby chest of drawers; I was bent double... finally, I put the box under my arm and, still coughing, left that mausoleum of Goya family junk for only slightly fresher air.

Mariano:

Now is the time for people such as I: not slogging over books, but with a broad vision, not spending hours praying on their knees but living a life of refinement – that brilliance, that polish is impossible to counterfeit, impossible to falsify.

When I drive along the streets of Madrid, I know that recognition, fame and money are just waiting for me. I am young, I am handsome, I have a beautiful wife with excellent connections in the best commercial spheres – and now it is merchants, not grandees, who will dictate the law, though it is also worth trying one's best for a title – I have a better name than many a marquis, especially among the new ones, the Marquises of Loyalty, the Marquises of Fidelity, whose fathers often worked in the fields and ate grass out of sheer hunger. The most important thing is to get a firm foothold somewhere now, to enter the appropriate circles, dance with the right ladies at the right balls, at the right end of the ballroom, under the right chandelier. The rest will take care of itself.

Javier:

The brushes were laid out in perfect order: all the paints had dried up by now, but the pigments, which I found in the studio, still shone with pure colours, just as they had thirty years ago. I told Felipe to cover the table, then I sent him to the city with a shopping list, to don Millares, whose father and grandfather provided the old boar with paints, oil and canvas, and had supplied Mengs and Tiepolo before him; and then I went upstairs to have a bite to eat.

I sat down by the window, from where I could see the line of the Manzanares, the neighbouring property right on the riverbank, the washerwomen sitting on stones like a flock of hens, and above them the city, its towers and cupolas, its stone walls glowing in the sunlight of early afternoon, like the bones of a giant, occupied by vermin. Vermin driving their own carriages, vermin buying and selling, flowing in whole streams over the ground, stealthily penetrating their burrows, digging the dark corridors of their nasty enterprises; a corpse occupied by hatching maggots, an old ruin full of cockroaches.

Closer to hand spread our land, which the old badger had so doggedly cultivated: a small vineyard, rows of apple and cherry trees, beds where at one time fine-looking leeks and huge artichokes had grown; how badly it had all deteriorated over the years when there was no one to take care of the harvesting or the irrigation; here and there poles stuck out of the scorched earth, up which something used to climb, something had once twined its grasping green whiskers; nothing hung there now but tangles of dried-up stalks and leaves. The rows of fruit trees had been thinned out: here a tree had been snapped in two by the wind, there another had been chewed by the hares which came at night, sometimes right up to the house; elsewhere Felipe or one of his predecessors had forgotten to do the watering for such a long time that the trees had withered to woodchips, to ashes. Only the poplars kept going somehow, and even in the almost standing air one could see their light, silvery rippling. Mariano had wanted to establish something new there – first of all to level the ground and create an English park, then to restore the garden and orchard again to look the same as in the old man's day, then to build a picturesque artificial ruin there; changeable, restless all the time, he couldn't make up his mind. So that's how it looked – in one spot at the edge a little earth had been brought in, elsewhere some small trees had been planted to replace the old ones, which had shrivelled away and had to be dug up; but the new ones had been forgotten too, and had met exactly the same fate. Near the shed a pile of stones had been heaped up from a run-down monastery, two columns and a few artificially shaped boulders, which were gradually settling into the ground. It was all wild, with no rhyme or reason. Great appetites and feeble willpower – that's what we are made of.

Now, I thought, as I gazed at an artichoke heart, we even have to buy artichokes. In the middle of the season. Yet so many used to grow here, and such handsome ones. And we were going to set up a cheese dairy too, that would have been something; if the old badger had stayed in Spain he would have changed this place out of all recognition. How fortunate that he didn't manage it. I liked this atmosphere of neglect and abandonment, the crooked shed, the jagged rows of trees, the miserable vines. I pushed my chair away from the table, leaned my head on my hands and, more and more drowsy, gazed out at that boldly uncultivated wilderness, a monument to idleness, the role entrusted to those spiteful gardeners, the wind and the torrid heat. What wonderful abjection.

I was only woken by Felipe, making a terrible racket as he hauled off a handcart and lugged across the threshold boxes, large bottles and crates containing everything I had ordered from Millares; I opened my eyes, turned my stiffened neck, wiped my lips, on which I could still taste a very fine layer of olive oil, and got to my feet. "Javier," I said to myself, "there's work ahead of you."

Though at the time I still hadn't the slightest idea what actually lay ahead of me.

I stood in a corner of the drawing room on the ground floor, braced myself a bit and moved the sofa away from the wall to avoid spattering it; I laid some cloths from the old boar's studio on the ground – naturally, he was never bothered about soiling, dirtying, smearing, staining or getting anything muddy; he splashed and splattered paint over everything, and held three brushes in one hand, using one to paint, and constantly scraping the other two now against his own clothing, now against a picture drying nearby; my mother wouldn't let him out across the threshold of the studio with a brush. That was what they had agreed between them, and amazingly, he abided by this custom until the day she died; only then did he grow audacious, setting up his easel or engraving equipment in any old spot; it all had to be cleaned afterwards, when we rebuilt the house for the young ones. Even that Weiss woman couldn't keep him under control – in Bordeaux everything was stained. Filthy.

I took off my frock coat and rolled up my shirt sleeves. I went out into the courtyard and there I mixed water and plaster in a small pail; I don't know what the old man threw into the plaster under his frescoes – he had his own recipes; I simply added a lot of lead white, the same stuff which according to my uncle had poisoned so many little boys and girls in the Goya family, and changed their hesitant brothers and sisters into freaks and slimy shreds, landing on the bloody bedclothes; I wanted the underlay to be luminous. And then, with Felipe's help, I brought in the pail, suddenly heavy, full of matt white, and smelling of wet earth, after which, as if it were the most ordinary thing in the world, I dipped a broad trowel in it, and from end to end plastered over a broad strip of the golden calico, printed with tiny flowers. And then a second one. And there was more furniture shifting, and so on. I worked like a madman, but that was just the start, that was nothing. Flat white surfaces without a single mark, under which the invisible, tiny pattern was still vibrating. Rosebuds.

Mariano:

We were not in Madrid at the time – Concepción and I had gone on a little journey to take in a bit of the great world; and thus Paris. Anyone who has never poked his nose beyond the Pyrenees has no idea what real life is like! There it is as bright as day in the middle of the night; in Spain, when the benighted populace didn't like the reforms of the minister who banned long overcoats and *sombreros*, in two days flat four thousand streetlamps were destroyed, which he had had erected all over the city, and the guardsmen had their tongues ripped out and their eyes gouged out, and their cut-off heads were carried about the city on pikes, each one wearing a huge *sombrero*. Grandfather was young then, but to this day we are sitting in the very same darkness.

We played – we played hard: at cards, at dice, on the violin, on the viol! I fought a duel over Concepción's honour, and she was delighted – she touches the scar on my thigh as if it were a holy relic. We bought plenty of scores – Haydn, Beethoven. Apparently Boccherini is completely out of fashion now; well, Paris dictates everything, and fashion never stands still just because someone isn't following it. One especially lovely

German piece for a trio, from Probst, is superb – the notes have a very readable shape. By a man called Schubert, opus 100 – most evidently a prolific composer, but they didn't have many more of his pieces there, they say he's no longer alive, he died the same year as Grandfather. Just think, so many years have gone by, and I can still see Señora Weiss before my eyes, saying: "He died as if he'd fallen asleep... even the doctor... was surprised how much... how much strength he had in him... they say he didn't suffer" – and that faltering voice – "but it's not true... not true" – and that tripping on the completely smooth floor.

Violin, cello and piano – how much refined simplicity there is in this – the beautiful second movement, which we are now learning. Concepción says that while playing it, she can feel a strange current in her fingers, as if she had plunged her hands into Mesmer's *baquet*. Don Rodrigo laughs at her, but as he draws his bow across the strings, he too has a look of suffering on his face. Outside it is already dark, there are three candlesticks by the music stands, and every murmur is audible. First the rattle of the piano – Concepción. Then don Rodrigo on the cello: tam tam tataaa-dam, tara ta-ra taaam, tata-daaam... As if something were knocking at our lives, at my life. And cannot enter. But straightaway in comes the violin – I raise my bow and wait for my bar.

XXVIII

Javier:

Only now, as I worked patiently for three days to cover all the panels between the doors and windows in plaster, and to whitewash all that *delightful* golden calico, which my daughter-in-law had insisted on having, did I start to wonder why am I doing this? Couldn't I start with an ordinary little picture, one foot by one and a half? There I sat, wiped out, on a stool draped in an old cloth, amid all those pieces of furniture, which until now had seemed to create a certain whole, an inviolable one in fact: the long table and twelve chairs upholstered in green damask, the mahogany corner tables with marble tops, the bureau which has always stood at the centre of one of the longer walls... ever since the old badger moved his sett here they have had their permanent places, they've always been the same distance apart, like points on a map; meanwhile it has turned out that with altogether not much effort it was possible to destroy this empire of bits of junk in a single afternoon, and to cast over their heads – in other words, backrests, tops and crowns – a pile of old cloths, and then regard them with a completely different eye. Here we have a flock of beggars, trailing off to San Antonio de la Florida on the day of the parish fair, at first light (the sun is already setting and is standing low, and its long streaks and long shadows are cutting right across the room; it's easy to imagine it is only just dawning, but from the other direction); they're all but trembling in eager anticipation of alms; the small card table is one of those legless veterans who shifts along on a low cart; the bureau is a blind fat man, being guided by the fire screen, a skinny ten-year-old, whom he is already training for the profession. A disorderly little crowd, hurrying up to the church steps, it has come to a halt, captivated by the dark-orange light gleaming from behind the houses, and is now warming itself in the sun's rays, for although it is June, the nights can still be cold. Or a family fleeing Zaragoza to escape from the French. The sofa is a cart carrying the remains of their possessions, plundered by soldiers; the horse has been shot along the way, so at the shaft there are two brawny sons (that's the bureau; they're so close together that they're merging into one), behind it there are several chairs – the younger children, little starvelings lugging bundles, and an old hag, there has to be an old hag too. Hunch-backed. Oh, we'll put a small stool on the card table and cover it with a cloth again. And beyond the hill of the table, as yet invisible, stand the soldiers, who will slaughter the lot of them, in the orange glow emanating from the burning city.

What used to seem so secure, the festive order of the drawing room, now stands before me in despair, groaning. Put us back against the walls. Around the table. In the corner. The same one as ever, no other. But there is no going back to the old corners, Javier is having a minor revolution.

I could have primed a nice little canvas for myself. Or a sheet of copper – there were still some of the old man's copper plates left; I could also have painted on one of those plates, on which he had etched *Los Disparates*, but that will keep for some time yet, to make prints and sell them; I'm not going to throw money out of the window like Rosario. I could – for why not? – order some top-quality canvas from don Millares – ha, I wouldn't have to do a thing to it, they'd stretch, glue and prime it all for me themselves, then polish it as smooth as can be as well, and be happy to do it. They'd be just as I wished, from tiny right up to bigger than those long, as yet empty friezes that stretch the length of both drawing-room walls. But I prefer to ruin the calico chosen by my daughter-in-law. I prefer to do it in here, where the old man used to receive his guests, where I lost at cards so many evenings, and so many copper coins – we never played for higher than *maravedís* – and where I had to watch that serpent Weiss winding herself around the old man, squeezing everything she possibly could out of him. And now they're all going to come here – those who are no longer alive, those who cannot enter this house in body, but are all too eager in soul, and those who enter it in body and soul, to chew on something fresh, make some music, and play cards, for why not? or have a drink – people like a drink too. And it's not as if they're going to walk up to some little picture hanging in the corner, or at least to a large picture, covering an entire wall, and mutter some comment; no, they'll be sitting inside the picture. Enough drudgery, since Mariano has insisted on converting this ordinary little house into a palace of clay, let it be a palace through and through, fit for the dukes of Osuna, let it be like Alba's, like La Granja. I may be no expert on tapestries, but old Javier is probably still capable of painting something pretty.

And so I sit there, without moving from the spot. I can smell the odour of drying plaster, like the damp inside of the earth, where my father has long since decomposed, along with his Franciscan habit and the little ebony cross which Gumersinda placed in his stiffened fingers, along with every bead in his rosary, and I gaze at the walls. The ones I plastered first are going white; the grey stains and damp patches have disappeared from them, as from a bone, baked by the sun at its zenith; those on which I have only just been working are merely flat, grey surfaces in plaster frames. The most curious are yesterday's: they look as if something has already been painted on them, but has faded. Or been whitewashed, to cover up some shameful scenes, repulsive scenes, scenes that prompt shivers and vomiting. For instance showing a cruel, deaf father, hurling insults, the full horror of which he may not realize, for he is incapable of hearing them, and his cringing son. That stain, oh, there – isn't it a wonderful boy's head? Buried in his shoulders?

Mariano:

A letter came from my mother, saying that my father had set about some refurbishments at the house left by my grandfather – apparently he was painting the ground-floor drawing room – so let him paint, as long as it is bright and pleasant; though to my mind he should really focus on the garden instead – extend the avenue of poplars, regulate the stream to make it irrigate the whole property, as it used to; maybe create a picturesque English park, sloping gently down to the river? One could buy up the neighbouring estate, level it to the ground or rebuild it into a small mediaeval castle; it's all the rage in France now. The drawing room was as it was; obviously, it's a provincial place – here we'd be laughed at for all that calico; the curtains, the wallpaper and the patterns – in Madrid not even a prince would ever get himself what the average banker has in Paris. But then they pay through the nose for it. Oh, if only one could furnish a house in Madrid in the Parisian style! And have the Quinta del Sordo as one of those suburban manors. Rebuild it slightly, hide the hideous bricks, maybe make it an attic higher or add a mansard, and maybe a wing for regularity? Bring in furniture, curtains, everything, right down to the firedogs, right down to the saltcellars – now that would be something!

It's not so bad if he goes crazy in the drawing room; worse if he gets going upstairs, and God forbid, tells Felipe to remove the instruments from in there. Or sets about it himself, the fat fool, grabs Guarnieri's violin or Ortega's viol in those sausage-like fingers of his – anything can enter old Fatso's noddle. That should be taken care of at any cost.

Javier:

There I sat the whole evening and came up with nothing, so I set about plastering the wallpaper in the large study upstairs; there used to be beautiful wallpaper from the Royal Factory in there, stamped using large plates, all hunting scenes and landscapes – one of the few extravagances Mariano allowed himself for his wedding party; he himself rarely hunted and did it rather badly, but he remembered his grandfather, whose eye was no good and whose hand shook – despite which, every few days he went to "have a bit of a shoot, to keep in practice" – so instead of following in the old man's footsteps, going after hares and missing, he bought wallpaper with a hunter bringing down a hare from the opposite corner of the room. But Concepción thought it hideous, and bought some cheap English tat, printed with a roller. Brown grapes on a trellis, with large, dirty-green leaves. Can one imagine anything uglier?

I preferred not to touch Mariano's instruments; I simply surrounded them with chairs and other furniture just as they were, as Napoleon did the scholars and donkeys beneath the pyramids, and covered them all at once; a mountain of Goya family furniture, large and egg-shaped – moss grew over the violin and the chairs, the wind carried sand and earth into the grand piano's case and sowed lush plants in there, time changed the wood into rot and the metal into rust. I can already see how in a hundred years there won't be a trace of us left here, just a small heap of stones. Dried in the sun, the brickwork will crumble to fine powder, and maybe just the remains of the monastery that Mariano had brought here to build a romantic ruin will be in a slightly better state, and some scholar will think to himself, what a lovely abbey must once have stood on this mound of rotting wood.

In any case, now I have fifteen empty fields – six downstairs, four smaller, two bigger, and nine upstairs, four bigger, four smaller and one tiny *supraporte* facing the stairwell. All blank, all from grey to white, from damp to dry. And still not a single idea.

Nothing vile, nothing repulsive. None of the images that lie in black layers in my head – no blood, toothless jaws, demons, soldiers, none of the things the old tomcat poisoned me with for all those years, that he trickled through my eyes into my brain. No garrotte, no French soldiers making fast, spasmodic movements between a pair of white thighs (the face is not visible, it is hidden by the raised skirt), no bull's horns piercing through soft flesh, through delicate layers of tissue; none of those things.

Something pleasant. A landscape. Mountains, a river glittering on a bend, stapled by the spans of a stone bridge. Trees moving in the wind. Lots of lush greenery (Felipe will have to be sent to the store for a large portion of green clay) – perhaps an occasional figure; a little shepherd, lost in the broad landscape, a peasant dancing at a village entertainment, a traveller on a mule – maybe a priest with his breviary, maybe a petty tradesman, clutching his saddlebag in horror? No, no horrors. Just a tradesman, riding an ordinary mule. That's it. A priest, a breviary. Three spans of the bridge and the silver bends of the river.

Mariano:

Fatso has started to grow eccentric. Old age. Concepción sent me to the Quinta del Sordo to check what was happening with the instruments; in any case, I was just as worried about them as she was. So I drove up, and from the threshold onwards there was a dreadful mess, in the drawing room and the music room everything had been moved about, thrown in a heap, my boots got tangled in the cloths laid all over the floor along the walls; in the corridors and on the stairs there were pails, bags, and sticks for mixing paint scattered under foot, spread about by Felipe anywhere and everywhere... Terrified, I dashed upstairs – luckily neither Fatso nor that blockhead had dared to lay a finger on the instruments or move them; they had just surrounded them with furniture like a palisade and covered them with sheets. I called Felipe to help me, and carefully, cautiously, we put everything back again, managing not to damage the viols or the violin. And then, with the greatest care, I extracted them from under the piano, I wiped off the dust, put them in their cases and, fearing that Felipe would do them harm, I carried them in person, looking closely under foot to avoid stepping in a pail or a jar, into the next room, which I locked, and attached the key to my watch chain, since when I guard it like a jewel. Unfortunately, nothing could be done with the piano; it had to remain in the middle of that mad chaos – I merely made sure they covered it so that neither dust not paint could get inside or stain the polish, and, sweaty and quite angry, yet also quite relieved, I went back to Madrid. There I still had to hear out my own share of it from Concepción, who started asking questions about what exactly my father was painting over. When she found out it was her favourite gold calico that she had chosen before our wedding, she had a fit of hysteria and told me to return to the Quinta del Sordo that very evening and – as she put it – "explain to my dunce of a father that if he wanted to scrawl on the walls he could do it in his own house, but not in the house I had been left by my grandfather". I wriggled and writhed to convince her it was too late now for another, evening drive out of the city; it took an effort to persuade her, but next day she was still nagging away at me to "go there and sort out that fat fool once and for all". But I have neither the time nor the nerves for that – ultimately I even sympathize with him in a way. He dashes about both rooms or up and down the stairs painting trees and bushes. It's dark and sombre, there's no taste in it at all, here a rock, there a cloud – my grandfather used to entrust this sort of background to various good-for-nothing pupils when he was in a hurry with the next picture. He raises that bloated, pug-dog face of his to look at me and says: "Marianito, look how nice it's going to be, just think how pleased Concepción will be, even she... just imagine coming here with your guests to make a little music, and instead of all that calico you'll have lovely things, views on all sides, as if there were twice, three times as many windows, and as if you could see the Manzanares through all of them, the washerwomen by the water, and the trees... the countryside, peace and quiet, a cool breeze – what a pleasure it will be to make music in such an interior. An enormous pleasure. You leave the city, the noise, the dirt and the tumult, and here," – and he makes a movement like an obese ballerina in a painter's smock – "you have an idyll..."

"All right, all right," I said, "do your painting, Father."

Javier:

The whole idea is still unclear. I know it's not yet there. But when Mariano came, I think he was delighted with what he saw, with what is already there to be seen. A wealth of colours and different times of day – I think even he understands what a joy it will be to come here from the city and play instruments among these lucid landscapes; because this is the real Spanish countryside, the scent of sun-baked stone, a mountain in the distance, a city under a storm cloud, a peasant doing a folk dance under a leaning tree. But it's not there, not there yet – some of the frames are still entirely empty, or barely covered in faint drawings, others are almost filled to the edges. I am not capable of painting each picture separately; anyway it's often impossible, the paint has to have time to dry, so I keep moving from one wall to another, from the ground floor to the first, I run upstairs and down, unsatisfied. I do not know what to grab hold of first, and what later, and clearly I am showing it, because when Gumersinda came here from Madrid she was seriously worried about my health and wondered if she should sent Doctor Díaz here soon. But I recognize it, and so does she – once, years ago, she saw how I painted *The Colossus* with the same sort of intensity – an incomparably smaller picture, of course; and now there are so many walls, so many scenes, so many subjects. When I get hungry – which I hardly feel, just a sudden spasm in my guts reminds me that I haven't eaten anything for a few, sometimes more than twelve hours – I sometimes sit by the window upstairs and gaze at the Manzanares. At the washerwomen, the carriages, a peasant carrying oranges on a handcart, to sell them later to the orange girls; and at the changing colours of the water, which at noon can be grey or greenish, but in the evening looks like a vein of gold within the darkened ore of fields and houses. And then I fly downstairs to a picture I have started, or not even that – I simply go up to the nearest wall and start painting what I have seen; the plumes of trees, capricious in the wind, or a man with a sack walking along a road. But I know the whole idea is still unclear. I know it's not yet there.

XXIX

The Holy Office

It starts with a dot, with a greenish, blackish drop of paint on the end of the brush – it has touched the wall, and is being smeared around and around, and keeps growing. It was only going to be just another leaf, ruffled by the first October wind, or a shadow cast by the canopy of a pine tree, rooted into the steep mountainside, but it is widening and changing into a black eye socket, spreading to become half a chubby face, wandering, emitting black earthworms – the shadow of broad lips and a nose, totally out of place here: loathsome, frequently licked by a wet, flickering tongue. Where does it think it's going, among the trees, the picturesquely wooded slopes, where does it think it's pushing its way into this canyon between the misty hills turning blue – that snout? And everything that comes with it to complete the set: around a muzzle like a rotting watermelon, around decaying oranges and sticky black – the dirty grey folds of the scarf, the dark dresses and the outline of a second figure; and now what was just one rebel drop is expanding into a second figure, into a stocky monk in a hood, showing his gorged belly like a monstrous pregnancy – no one knows what he has in there, perhaps the desire took him to give birth to a child, like Nero, into whose belly a frog was placed, and the frog grew and grew, until Caesar's doctors performed a Caesarian section and brought it into the light, I read about it as a boy in the lives of the saints from the library at the Piarists' school... and the one next to him... I can see my hand mixing a greenish yellow on the palette, which at once changes into a gold chain on a black costume, and shortly after I see how several mighty strokes create a square cross just above it, and then a thin brush draws the pointed tips of a bristling moustache and a wispy beard... the one next to him is indeed a doctor, a surgeon specializing in breeding frogs in the bellies of monks and Caesars who want to bear a child; behind him there's an evil spirit, whispering something into his ear about a plump, ageing man who is standing before a wall in just a smock and has no idea why he has introduced this entire suspicious company into an idyllic landscape.

These three – the old woman in the headscarf, the monk and the doctor – are looking at me closely. They are the Holy Office of the Inquisition, which came from who knows where, from the paint, from deep in the wall, from under the plaster and calico printed with little roses, and now they are judging me. And they are scowling, oh how they are scowling, curling their lips into a grimace, knitting their brows, clapping themselves on the belly, and tightly gripping a scroll with the sentence. And behind them, the ones who follow, a multitude, I see row upon row of them approaching, slowly trailing along the road: hunchbacked old hags, doctors, and judges in wigs, fat men, cripples, every one of them wants to come up and pass judgement on me.

You oaf, you clod, you slob, you fatso, they say, you layabout, you cringer, you parasite, you stinking idler, you impotent, you weakling, you weed, you amoeba, they say, you madman, you artist who has never painted a single picture, you horrible old man, you stinker, they say, you mistake, you trash, you mooncalf, you ordure.

The words come pouring from their large, puffy lips like a black river and flood the entire landscape, the picture, the next few pictures, and me; they climb the stairs to the first floor, flowing around the column with the massive head of my father; and lapping against it lovingly.

XXX

Javier:

It was already dark. It had already been dark for many hours now, for I had seen the shadows growing longer and longer as they were sent across the room, I had seen the light turning orange, and then grey, until finally it faded out. And I had seen myself, tripping over a pail as I went to fetch a candelabra, as I set it by the wall on a side table swathed in cloths, and as I lit the candles. But I couldn't feel that it was I at all, I felt as if it were someone else, someone who had arrived at the empty house in my absence, crept up, smashed the lock and noiselessly come up the stairs and was painting over my pictures, spoiling them, scrawling on them, splashing them with paint, daubing, extracting from the viscous layers old hags wrapped in headscarves, the great belly of a monk, dresses and overcoats, hideous ugly faces. I could see him labouring to paint a processional flag, then giving up and cursing, as he changed it into a reddish rock, which had tumbled down from the invisible mountain top, looming somewhere above from time immemorial, as with swift strokes of the brush he multiplied the crowd, head after head, like dark scales on the back of a predatory fish.

I did not know him. I did not know that self, I had forgotten him – he had been sleeping for all this time. It was he, all those years ago, sitting in an armchair over a volume of poetry in green marbled covers, who in a single flash had seen the mighty Colossus, rising out of the mists above the battling armies. And it was he who painted him, in a state of oblivion, and then vanished. He went down the stairs into Calle de los Reyes, shut the door behind him and only reappeared today, in my smock, and in my breeches, with my thinning hair on his head; he opened the door down below and, just as if he knew the way, came straight up the stairs to the first floor, went over to the wall, took the palette from the side table, mixed green and black, and put one single dot on the landscape, from which it all began, from which it all developed. I watched all this, dumbstruck, and then I went up to him. And we merged into one.

XXXI

Seizure

I? Me? I do not even look like myself, but I can feel that it is me you are carrying away on a boat made of wind, on air-borne wings, and I can feel my smock changing into a coat billowing with gusts of air and, locked together – you are holding me by the elbow with such strength that sometimes I think you will tear off my arm – we are gliding above a vast battlefield.

Yes, now I remember it all: air, hunger, fire and war. Nothing has escaped me, nothing has passed me by, for even if I didn't see it with my own eyes, with my eyes closed I saw it somewhere deeper down, with the second pair of eyes that each of us has, even if he tries to cover them. Or gouge them out. Legs – the legs the door bumped into as I left the house at dawn, I no longer remember what for, just the thump, as if wood were striking wood; for they were as thin as sticks, as crutches, as canes – in those days one saw many legs like those, and many arms like those, hands like bundles of brushwood, faces like fruit stones, with the skin pulled tight – and a body at the end of the legs, emaciated, wrapped in rags, with the head drooping and the eyes still open; I stopped, surprised, and tried to gaze as he was gazing, at what he was gazing at, and I saw a piece of bread gripped in his fingers, a piece of bread given by someone merciful, maybe even by our cook, enclosed in a hand which could not raise it to his mouth – but now a thin child crawls up to the clenched hand, like a dog, like a dog with a damaged spine, and reaches for the bread, greedily, snatches it, as if for a sudden moment it had gained strength, devours it and stops still. Now it will digest. It is unable to go further, it cannot go further. Oh, I have seen it all. I have seen burning cities and women with their legs tied to two stakes, like a split-open sow, on top of whom five, ten, fifteen of them lay, until the last one slashed her with a broadsword from breast to crotch. I have seen what metal can do to flesh, what shells and bayonets can do to flesh, sharpened knives too, and farmers' pitchforks, and a cast-iron fence post, with a bound prisoner spiked on it. But I closed both pairs of eyes, because I preferred not to look, not to poison myself with those sights, for I was deluding myself that it is possible to avoid being poisoned.

And now I can see it again, I can see it plain as day: foreign troops ravaging the land, people carrying saddlebags full of cut-off French ears with ear-rings and cut-off French fingers with rings, and I can see people crucified on barn doors, and trees with their branches breaking under the weight of hanged men; I can see horses whose flesh in collision with metal has just as slim a chance as human flesh, and I can see barrels pointing, greasy with lubricant, oiled with dense black, bone-black. You have opened my eyes to all this, lifting me up on your air-borne sail, on the rearing wind.

I do not know you and I will never know you; your face is veiled by the thick, red cape, in which you are muffled from knees to nose – here, in the heights, there is no tree, no wall to shield us from the icy wind that blows across this hostile land, raising leaves, shreds of clothing, smoke and wind-borne travellers. I can see your hair and eyes and brow, but you do not have who you are written on your brow, you do not have your name written on your brow – you may be a demon and a goddess, you may be an allegory incarnated in a live, warm body, wrapped in scarlet cloth, in any case no one ordinary, for whence could you have flown? This is not the flight of a country witch who sits her withered thighs, smeared in lard from a hanged man, astride a fire-iron or a broomstick, oooh, this is an entirely different flight. I? Me? Carry me off to this dangerous plain, to this wild mountain with the city that will defend itself against any army, with a cathedral, towers, and granaries rich in corn, dried meat and fruits? Carry me above the flying bullets and put me down there, to do something useful at last at the end of my life? And if not useful, then beautiful? Asmodeus embodied in a woman? Minerva? Art? Oh, seize me, carry me away, so beautifully do you carry me away!

XXXII

Mariano:

My mother was the first to alert me. She came to visit, had only taken off her hat and, still on the doorstep, with the pins from her chignon in her hand, she said: "Your father is not well". And when was he ever well? When, I say? Doesn't she remember how he used to lie about in corners, in armchairs, how she used to send the maid to him with a glass of herbs, sighing to me: "The shrinking violet needs watering"? Doesn't she remember how he wouldn't say a word for days on end, how he'd fall into a sudden frenzy if she said: "Javier, get out of the house because you're growing a coat of moss", until he foamed at the mouth? How he used to talk to flies and mice? What does "not well" mean in this case?

But let her have it her way – I promised to go to the Quinta del Sordo on Friday, because this constant drone of complaints has reduced me to a nervous wreck. She sat in an armchair with a cup of stone-cold, congealed chocolate and lamented that she hadn't seen him in this state for years, that she didn't recognize him at all, that he had changed horribly, that he looked unwell. So I arrive, and Fatso's in an excellent mood, ruddy, full of excitement, sitting outside the house at a heavily laden table, devouring a mountain of food: olives, peppers, bread, fried fish, pears, all at once. "Well," I think to myself, "at most he'll get a bit fatter, but the floor won't collapse under him – not in vain did we reinforce it before my wedding. But to me he doesn't look like a sick man. He's talking about local matters, about some farmhand from the neighbours, about a milkmaid, about how Felipe scratched his arms pruning branches, how the cat had kittens, spraying sauce as he talks, spitting crumbs – the tablecloth is covered in stains and lumps of spat-out food. I can see my mother has just been having yet another fit of complaining and lamenting – now I want to get out of here, as if I am just passing through, but my father drags me inside to show me how he has prepared our rooms. "I have fully populated them," he says, "they're finally alive – none of those boring trees or bridges, this is real painting" – and he pulls me by the sleeve. So I follow. "All right, Father," I say, "all right, I'm coming."

And from the drawing-room threshold I realized my father was not well. Not well at all. Where last time there were some ineffectual landscapes, peasants on mules, rivers, all that stuff, now there are clusters of goblins, repugnant figures, devils, witches, old hags that make one want to vomit. I saw a distillation of my grandfather's worst nightmares: glowing bodies plunged in a thick mass of black, as in condensed ink; ravaged plains and hideous, twisted faces. The worst of all the shapes on earth, which finally opens to take them in, although they make it feel nausea, and a sudden tremor runs through the rocks. "Father," I asked, "what is it?"

"What is it? It's the truth."

Javier:

The longer I painted, the more I could see my ineptitude. The least successful pictures I completely painted over: I took thick paint from the pail and again, and again, in broad stripes

I laid the background, then I picked out the light in white, and so the shapes emerged, doubly – from light to shadow and from darkness to penumbra. Penumbra is truest of all, and thus hardest to paint – light and dark are easily rendered, but in penumbra every scrap of the picture creates almost unlimited possibilities.

I reworked other scenes, hacked off a bit of plaster, laid it again, applied a little paint, smoothed it. Never enough, I never had enough of it: scratch off this face and illuminate it again, sharper yet; here do something with the robes, because they look suspicious. Here add a fold, smooth out the edge of a sleeve, add a building on the horizon, give someone a hunchback, if he needs it. And there are some who need it. I kept approaching some of the walls over and over, at various times of day and night, now talking to myself, now asking the visitors' opinion, at longer and shorter intervals, sometimes day after day, another time without returning to the painting in question for a whole fortnight.

I felt alive – I could see how the weather was changing outside, how the summer was ending and ever more often there was a gust of cold in the evening, and I had the feeling that I was part of that cycle, that I was dying, in order to be born, then that I was being born again, in order to die. Now I was being born, I was being born with all the pores of my skin, I was being born through my nostrils and my buttonholes, through my fingers, through my navel. Now at last the wind from the Pyrenees had reached me – so many years had it taken to bring the news of my father's death from Bordeaux.

Mariano:

I told Concepción we shall never set foot there again,

our children even more so – that was all we needed, for little Mariano Javier and María de la Purificación to see those monstrosities capable of causing the most detestable superstitions and madnesses to hatch in their young, unformed minds, still soft as the kernel of a walnut.

Naturally Concepción demanded that I throw my father out of La Quinta, order all the pictures to be hacked off and have the walls covered in material again, but a more elegant kind than in the days of our engagement. In the end, in theory it is my land and my house. Anyway, I can already imagine his rage if anyone were to dare to damage those *masterpieces* by Javier Goya, the painter without a single picture to his name – though since recently with a certain number of daubs.

And yet, as I lay in bed at night, trying to sleep, the scenes I had seen there kept coming back to me in all their repulsive splendour: faces like masks, clouds hanging low, the black silhouette of a devil-goat in flowing robes, a small dog's head right by the frame. So is this what the sleep of reason produces?

Javier:

I was unsure of some of the fantasies, and kept wavering – first I would paint the background, then I would draw some hesitant lines and paint over them again. Another day it would come to me as easily as it had with that first drop, from which the entire procession of inquisitors had grown; idea came racing after idea, while that other Javier, stronger and sharper than I, wielded the brush with such speed and mixed the paints with such fervour that I couldn't keep up with him; often my hand slipped from the intended outline, until I stopped it in embarrassment, and looked to see if it definitely was still my hand, and not a living tool being controlled by someone else's will.

The end was still far away, but somehow I was getting closer to it.

XXXIII

The Duel

Every war is a war about space; great empires send hundreds
of regiments to their death, burn down cities and fields of
unreaped corn, raze monasteries to the ground, hack down
orchards and slaughter flocks, just to have even more room –
because those heraldic beasts, the lions of León, the eagles of
France, need a great deal of space to gorge themselves to the
full; but a man knows nothing about war, about all-consuming
hatred, or about battling to the last drop of blood until he has
seen two Aragonese or Galician peasants fighting over a piece
of land. For even when empires are battling against each other,
right down at the very bottom, beneath the unfurled banners,

beneath the trails of cannon smoke, beneath the pyramid of ranks and titles, beneath the brightly coloured cloth and gold buttons of the uniforms is a Galician peasant, sticking his bayonet into the belly of a peasant from Picardy, or a swineherd from Fuendetodos, using his broadsword to hack off the arm of a Gascon miller in the fight for a strip of boundary four fingers wide.

Torrential rain has already fallen on the ground; on the left one can see a foaming, fitful river; from among the dark grey clouds shines a patch of clear sky, which, if looked at closely, is like the profile of a mighty lion, gazing at a steep mountain in the distance; nothing is left of the storm but mud; it stretches from the hills to the low, slushy water, so much mud that there's enough for everyone. They are both standing up to their knees in it, belabouring each other with cudgels. Without fury, without sudden rage: instead they are methodically, consistently delivering blow after blow. The one on the right, the younger man, has shielded his mouth with his arm and is raising his brow in surprise; the one on the left, covered in blood that is pouring from his forehead and a ripped ear, seems equally surprised. In the brief moment, when their sticks have been drawn back by a swing of the arms and are only just gathering momentum to strike at an exposed forehead, a thick shock of hair, or at a hand, these two men are looking at each other, and are most evidently surprised that they have held out for so long, that instead of making it up, they keep on battering away, ignoring their wounds, and that they are fighting each other for space, though neither of them will give way, for neither is capable of giving way, tethered by the mud as if by snares.

As far as the eye can reach, there isn't a living soul. All this land is theirs, but they keep bogging themselves down deeper and deeper in the mud, eyeing each other up, as they plan the next blow to make it hurt as much as possible.

XXXIV

Javier:

Gumersinda appeared in person. What an honour. She brought
me some peaches from the city, saying they were so nice that
at once she had thought of me – as if we hadn't known each
other for more than twenty-five years, as if she really believed
I would let myself be taken in by such a ruse... We sat down
in the kitchen, for in the new wing, both upstairs, and on the
ground floor, all over the house everything was still moved
aside, the furniture was pushed into the middle, covered with
cloths, and on the floor there were pieces of hacked-off plaster
lying about, as well as lumps of paint that had fallen from the
jars, and bowls filled with dried-up flakes of red, green and
black; most of all black. So we sat here, in the kitchen. I, a
workman in stained, old breeches, with splashes of yellow on
my threadbare waistcoat, and patches of white stubble on my
cheeks; and she, an elegant woman – she always knew how to
spend the Goyas' money well; anyway, in all fairness one must
admit that she did pretty well at spending the Goicoecheas'
money too – in a dress of crimson satin, new, I think, though
I am not sure... but I didn't like to ask, so it wouldn't come
to the fact that I am not just an old lunatic but a miser too...
as well as that she was wrapped in a Scottish shawl, given to
her by Mariano. It was too warm for that shawl – even if the
carriage had raced like mad to the Manzanares she wouldn't

have been cold in this weather; as she came in, I saw tiny beads of sweat on her upper lip, quivering on the small dark hairs that have started to grow there. And on her forehead, yes, just below the hairline – she certainly hadn't been cold, but she wanted to show off that shawl. She watched as I cut up peach after peach – not with a little fruit knife, as she would have wished, but with the ordinary pocket knife I sometimes use to scrape paint off the palette – while I observed her hands, as she arranged the shawl. Now to one side, now the other. She stands up, lets it drop low, so that it's hanging in the crooks of her elbows – how hot she's getting under her bodice, I thought, as it widens by the year – then she raises the shawl again, covering her shoulders. She's getting hot there too. She lowers the shawl. She raises it. And I'm slicing a fourth peach for myself, as if nothing were wrong, for in any case I know I'm supposed to be taking notice of the shawl – bah, I know she came about something else too, except that she doesn't know how to start. But she'd been sitting at home, in Madrid, on tenterhooks, itching all over, she'd stood up, sat down, stood up again, until finally she thought of those peaches. And what on earth for, I ask myself, since it's just the same here too – she keeps standing up, sitting down, standing up, sitting down. It's a shame to tire the horses and wear out the carriage axles just for that. I'm about to eat the last piece and say: "Well, spit it out then, woman!", but as I swallow it and toss the stone onto the plate, I hear: "Leocadia has returned to Madrid. With Rosario. And with the son."

Am I supposed to feel pangs of conscience now? I don't think that's what she came about. She's sure to have come with her own pangs of conscience, which do not concern me in the least. "Apparently they were living in awful poverty there. Rosario was keeping herself and her mother by doing little bits of work. She was teaching drawing, and painting miniatures on commission. And patterns on wallpaper."

Well, if you please – what perfect harmony. What a fine coincidence. She was painting patterns on wallpaper, and I was painting on wallpaper. I mention it, but Gumersinda is not amused. Not in the least bit.

"Lovely shawl," I say. She says it's from Mariano, that even now he remembered, despite the death of little Marianito. I say that we may only have one son, but he is exceptional. May her tormented soul find some rest. Shut inside her body, with its wrinkles, its whiskers and its beads of sweat.

Mariano:

I called my son Mariano Javier, just to please Fatso. What a fool I was. A name is no laughing matter. I could have called him Mariano Francisco, and maybe then he'd have had more of his great-grandfather in him. Strength and talent. I infected him with a name, like with gangrene, I killed him the day the priest poured water over his little head and baptized him Mariano Javier; how on earth did he come to be more like his grandfather than his father? Quiet, feeble, as if already withering in his cradle – no, there was no hope for him. Apparently children are generally more like their grandparents than their parents; for didn't what women have always liked so much about me come straight from the great Francisco de Goya? That style, that inner strength, the radiance of old-time nobility intensified by the radiance of genius! If only the little one had inherited that from his great-grandfather. And from me, honours and wealth, the former and the latter within arm's reach, ever closer; I have come upon news of some splendid deposits of silver in Peru, right by the surface – all that's needed is to build a small railway line across the mountains. On top of that, I now have my eye on two ancient grandees, one with gambling debts, the other vegetating in a half-collapsed palace, where his only company is a blind dog and a lame servant; three more months and both will sell me their titles for a song, for a hundredth of what Peru will bring me. And if not that, I am left with railways in the province of Aragon, where local speculations are bringing in tremendous profits, the peasants are selling land for nothing, and the railway is then buying it for a fortune. Ultimately my son-in-law could also take our surname, famed throughout Spain and beyond its borders; even if he's practically a stranger, then his children, my grandchildren, will still have the blood of the de Goyas in their veins.

Javier:

I looked at him in the cradle, and when he started to walk. "Where are you off to?" I'd say to him softly, or I'd repeat it to myself, "where are you off to, you silly little chap? Do you really want to tumble into that quagmire, onto that treadmill, where father poisons son, son – grandson, and grandson – great-grandson, each in a different, more sophisticated way; do you really want to prolong this line of suffering?" And now if you please, diphtheria. Not such a silly boy.

XXXV

Javier:

And yet this little death grieved me. And stuck inside me, when I awoke and when I went to bed, in the irregular rhythm of my work, eating, sudden naps and abrupt awakenings, when I felt as if something had grabbed me by the hair and was dragging me to the paints and brushes; in each of these separate moments that little death throbbed in my body like a festering splinter, like a piece of shrapnel.

It wasn't to do with mourning – I never had the chance to get used to him, and the fact that he was named after me did not mean much to me – but more with the awareness that he had weaselled his way out of all this, wriggled out, plopped into death like a white pebble into black, stagnant water; I simply envied him that – why hadn't I hit upon the same idea when I was like him: the size of a larva, small, pink and dribbling, fumbling in the dark, staring after anything at all.

How much simpler my life would have been: a few days, weeks, maybe months devoted to the work of my intestine. I would never have known my family, I would have been deaf to my relatives' words, and they would have been deaf to my babble. There'd have been none of those wives, fathers, children of my own, no love affairs and no pictures, no possessing, buying or selling; just being a short-lived intestine, which consumes, digests, and expires. And with me

Mariano would have disappeared, and Marianito too, and so many other people whom by improvidently remaining alive I have condemned to be born.

I painted on, envying him as I did so. I thought what would have happened if I had been like he was. Instead of standing at the wall, laying paint on it with a broad brush, I would have been occupied with lying motionless in a little coffin. The grubs would have teemed in my buttery flesh, millipedes would have passed through my eye sockets, centipedes would have run between my little bones. No one would have cared whom I resembled, I would not have passed on the likenesses of parents and grandparents to children and grandchildren, for I would only have resembled other decomposing bodies, all my brothers and sisters: Antonio, Eusebio, Vicente, Francisco, Hermengilda, and María de Pilar, who gorged themselves on lead white like poisonous sweets.

Not that I have painted every day. I don't have to, I don't live on it. I have days off. They start just like the industrious ones, with getting out of bed, and they end the same way too, with lying down in bed. No lounging in my litter with my gaze fixed on the wall. I have had my fill of staring at walls by now – both then, in the past, at a bit of cracked whitewashed plaster above the marital bed, of the happy young couple, Javier and Gumersinda, and now, as I take a close look at what's soon to disappear beneath the paint: smooth and rough patches, pockmarks and pores, which will be permeated, which will be sealed by shining wet green. So what else could I do, if not lie in bed and stare at the wall? I could do as the old man, cultivate the earth, inspect the artichokes, or go after birds, or hares. Mariano would be delighted if I took care of the orchard, the garden, did some shouting at the gardeners, the workmen, told them to dig ditches, to irrigate, build a fountain, plant rows of trees.

But I just walk about. Walking provides a lot of non-committal joy, even when it is as warm as of late, and a man is bound to puff and pant a bit, perspire a bit. I may not understand the fancies of the old man or the young one, all that business of making the earth subservient to you, all that converting, planting and cultivating, but I do understand the joy of walking around your own piece of land. My piece, I have it on paper. I can tell a stranger to get off my land. You're trampling on it, and I don't want that. I can walk around it with a stick in my hand, and I can wave the stick about, and look at the washerwomen by the Manzanares, at the fields, and at the city in the distance, gleaming in the sunlight like a heated chunk of limestone.

On days like this no one comes here. Generally no one ever comes here, not even on the industrious days, and if they do, there's Felipe standing in the doorway, who says the master is not here, or the master is busy, and that's the end of it; I can go on painting, unless it's Mariano or Gumersinda – for them I have to give way. Tear myself from the wall, come down the ladder, set aside my brushes, wipe off my hands. Keep an eye open to make sure they don't touch the fresh paint, best of all not let them into the new wing, or the ground floor, or upstairs. But on my days off no one has to be sent packing, absolutely no one at all, as if everyone were giving themselves that day off from Javier Goya, as if he had given himself a day off from the world, and the world from him. Then I can walk about the hills and fields, observe the lizards and the withering grasses. And stones. Every other stone has a face, though of course everyone is ashamed to admit it; they knew that in childhood, but then they became ashamed. The other stones have faces too, but they're more deeply hidden – just like people, not all of them are open. That was why I was so surprised that man came and found me on my day off, after my morning walk, after eating, when I had just got up from the table and was getting ready for my siesta.

He came in, out of breath, and without even introducing himself, he brought a large package from under his arm. "Here are the letters!" he said, as if giving me proof of something, as if delivering a verdict or an ultimate truth. And so I asked what letters, which letters, whose letters. "What do you mean, which? What do you mean, whose? Your father's to my uncle!" And he stares at me, blinking and squinting. For he has made another pronouncement. "I'm sorry," I say to him, wiping my hands on a napkin, "but with whom do I have the pleasure?" And again in that proclamatory tone, like a herald, like La Tirana treading the boards: "I am Francisco Zapater y Gómez, nephew of Martín Zapater!"

And indeed, I do remember, there was a man called Zapater, he died about thirty years ago, he sometimes used to come and hunt with the old man. They would ride off for a few days, now here, now there, do some shooting and go back home, one to Madrid, the other to Zaragoza.

"So you haven't read yours?" he asks, and glowers again, in amazement. "What do you mean, your what? My uncle's letters to your father. They must be somewhere. Either here, or in Madrid, for I know you have a house in Madrid too, I was there earlier, your wife sent me here. I have my ones, that is, your father's, and you have yours, that is, my uncle's. Unless he destroyed them. Could he have destroyed them? Before his death? Perhaps he destroyed them? Or maybe you destroyed your ones? Because mine are here. But what is to be done with them? Are they to be destroyed?"

He was a very lively man, and he spoke very quickly, incoherently to boot, shaking, squinting and spitting a bit, like a fairground puppet thrashing about on stage; I couldn't tear my eyes off him – first he threw out his arms, then he cringed, splayed his fingers, rolled them into fists... This house hadn't seen as much activity since Mariano's wedding.

"Destroyed?" I say to him. "What for?" But he plainly doesn't understand, he opens his mouth, closes it, pounds with his hands, curls up and uncurls: "Haven't you read them? Ha! Then please read them, sir, let's settle this like man to man!" Then he unpacks the letters and seeks one out, he clearly knows them extremely well, and has been through them many times. "If you please! If you please! And this one too! And this one. If you please!" He spreads them out in front of me, covering the entire table, on which shortly before I have been eating, around the plate, the glass, and the dish with a chicken quarter. He points at extracts. He covers one of the letters with a big drop of olive oil, which starts soaking into the paper, spreading to form a large, perfectly round stain.

Francisco:

+ *Jesus, what an enormous cock, God Almighty! You must have drawn around it with your pen while thinking about Little Miss Piety for if you drew it freehand you are a born artist and God alone knows it deserves framing as much as a saint deserves two candles. What a pity it can't be shown to the public for anyone to try it out and the lady it fits best could get to keep it. And what better subject for a portrait than a well-flogged bishop since no one can deny that without it the whole world would come to an end.*

I've just painted the robes and a cross made of precious

gems in my portrait of the Old Cow and today I got down to work on yours. How you must have laughed reading my last letter – it's a pity you're not here, what a good chat we'd be having! But at least you can sleep in peace without being disturbed by conversation for lately I haven't been chatting much which depresses me because I prefer your company to the moderate pleasures of stuffing my cock into birds' nests enough said.

Sod you, my friend! Your Paco likes you too much.

+ My Martín, your letters give me support, and if not for my duties as a painter I would come straight to you, for the feelings I have for you make it impossible for me to think about anyone else and I feel that we should always be together and go hunting and drink chocolate and happily blow the twenty-three reales I have on me in your company and that would be the most wonderful thing in the world (but what layabouts we would become!) but in reality all we can do in this world is to wish and when you write to me in that way I feel moved for hours to come, I talk to myself as if I were talking to you until at last I see that maybe I've been deluded and Fate is against it (I also think twenty-three reales would never be enough for our noble intentions.)

+ Dear Martín, I am happy to know that you're indulging yourself and that's exactly what I wish as you know and I don't have to say any more for you understand this perfectly and much more so there's no need to add anything. I'd love to see one of your fields which must surely be green by now. May it please God that we meet soon.

+ How much vigour there was in your last letter! Evidently

you can make anything up as you go along just as I can in my painter's imagination so keep writing to me! Send me that bill for my sister you old Devil, I've been waiting for it for so long now that if I didn't know you wouldn't be angry I'd return to you all she has had from you since you started sending her money and then I wouldn't owe anything which would make me very happy for when I think of it I can't rest and I sink into such a bad mood that it only passes once I've put a hand to my manhood. Are you laughing? well, do it yourself, do it, and at once you'll feel how much benefit it brings; you must do it, right now it's the season of evil thoughts, words and deeds at least according to my Aunt Lorenza who taught me these things – I must confess that at first I was terrified and confused but now? well now I'm not afraid of Witches, hobgoblins, phantoms, villains, Giants, rogues, scallywags, etcetera, nor any sort of body except human, and yours is the one your Goya loves the most.

+ ...And I offer everything to you with the joy with which one friend must give to another and boy both you and I know we are alike in everything and God has made us different from the rest, for which we should give thanks to Him for Whom anything is possible.

God be with you my dear friend whom I long to embrace. Your friend

Fat Little Paco

+ Had I not heard by chance that you are all but on your way to Madrid sir, I would have written to you, Honourable Sir, with due respect and style; but since I shall lose my respect for you as soon as you get here why don't I start now? So to put it bluntly I order you, since you'll have the opportunity to

enjoy the pleasure of serving me, to deliver this letter into the hands of the person to whom it is addressed and to inform me of the fact and by doing so sir you will delight me and at the same time I shall be doing a favour for a friend who is doing me a thousand favours (as ever). Quite simply: plenty of cock! Hurry sir, and come for we have to set tongues wagging. Dixi.

Prescription: Prick parsley bum; lambs in Caramanchel; Farlete; students' capes, then suddenly – a capon.

Javier:

"Indeed," I said, "these are my father's letters. His writing. He always put a small cross at the start, that's how they were taught at San Antonio's school."

"So did my uncle. And of course they're his. Who else's?" The little man had brought a chair up to the table for himself and sat on it, and now all his agitation, which earlier had also found an outlet in scraping his feet, jumping up and down, shifting his weight from one leg to the other and stamping, had to limit itself to the upper half of his body alone, which meant that he gesticulated even more violently, in rapid, fitful movements. "My uncle did the same, the same little crosses. Look here, sir: *my rogue*, here: *Gypsy of my heart*. And there: *All your Juanito of the Rutting or of the blue balconies*. And there are even worse bits. I'll find it all for you, I've been through it all already..."

He took out letter after letter, mixed them, unfolded and folded them again, and jabbed at the pages with his finger tip, until the timber of the table resounded. I asked him what he was thinking of doing with all this; I waited until he was done with his trembling, he came out with a few contradictory ideas, and I said: "Let me think it over in peace. I hope you can stay in

Manzanares until tomorrow. I'd offer you a bed for the night, but as you can see, the house is in the middle of being painted. I've heard that they have perfectly decent rooms at the Black Cockerel, and as for the cooking, I sometimes send Felipe there myself, to fetch me a small chorizo in red wine from them. But if they haven't a spare room, I'm sure you'll find something in the town itself." And I led him out, squirming, into the corridor, and from there, driving him on a little with some gentle arm movements, I steered him towards the door, just as one guides out a flapping butterfly that's beating its wings against the glass of a partly open window.

The letters were lying on the kitchen table just as we had left them: all higgledy-piggledy, one on top of another, around the plate, glass, empty wine bottle in a woven basket and the dish with the leftover chicken. I gathered them up carefully, told Felipe to clear the table, and then, with the wad of papers in my hand, I went into the room upstairs and sought out my father's bureau. In order to reach it, I had to pull a large cloth to the ground, then move aside about four chairs and a little table; finally I pulled up one of the chairs for myself and sat down at the folding desk top.

I tossed the letters onto the stained morocco leather and started to arrange them in order, one after the other; almost all were supplied with dates, and were written at speed, generally without commas, the full stops placed reluctantly, as if each sentence were going to be the very last and everything had to be contained in it: news of the death of a child, the purchase of a new gig, who shot how many hares and how many partridges, about his commissions and their commissioners, grumbling about old age and a request to send a bushel of corn flour, gossip about what Bayeu had heard from the Infantes about his picture, and above all money: investments, loans and prices.

Thirteen *reales* customs duty for a wineskin, fourteen for a bodice, which my mother sewed for Zapater's aunt, eleven for a parcel, ten doubloons for a pair of mules, one hundred and eleven *reales* as a loan, twenty-nine for a bushel of barley.

But only a blind man could fail to see what was going on between the words, and even in the words themselves, quite plainly and transparently, in the full light of day, as bluntly as could be – even if I didn't know why he had called himself Little Miss Piety or what he meant by a capon. Could the malady have harmed more than just his hearing? What did they get up to at Farlete and Carmanchel, and what did lambs have to do with it? Whence all of a sudden the blue balconies, and where did a man who never read poetry get the "Gypsy of my heart" from? But I could see that they had their own secret, affectionate language, where the point was that no stranger, from outside this world – in which hunting trips, hounds, dirty jokes, loud farting, folds of fat, coarse hair, and encounters between the body's protuberances and orifices all went together – that no stranger, who would lay their paws on these unburned letters after their death, would know what was meant by the capon and Farlete, and the students' capes, or where the tender words came from, which led to some evening only they knew about, some drunken joke, or strange incident on a journey. Students' capes? So it had already started then? How old was he in those days? The first letter... not quite thirty, ten years before my birth... he had left Zaragoza by then, he was back from Italy, he had married Mama, and yet between them, that fondling under the students' capes was still going on. And it went on like that for over twenty-five years. Just as if his entire life were a copperplate engraving: what we saw in black and white had its mirror equivalent, almost entirely black, with some fine lines of white.

But even if one didn't believe the words, there were drawings too. Between the lines, and in the margins around the signatures: a barber's bowl, a hound, a rifle and a hunter's saddlebag, with a hare's paws sticking out of it, a snake, a loaf of bread, cheese and bottles spread out on a blanket, but above all bodies: sometimes the bodies of men and women, but more often just men, twisted into disgusting poses, coupling like animals. In some of them I could recognize him: the sideburns, the thick hair parted in the middle, sometimes shorter, sometimes longer; I could see him getting older, how his body in the drawings was increasingly sagging and spreading, more and more like an overfed old badger, wolf, or bear. I also recognized that man, with a large, aquiline nose and thick eyebrows. And his gradual changes.

I was reminded of the scrawls from Bordeaux: a lustful bull with the tiny wings of a butterfly. Could I ever have thought he was drawing himself there?

I felt embarrassed, as if I'd gone into the bedroom and seen him there, naked, on the body of another man, sweaty, panting heavily, and then, as I sat facing the small drawers in his open bureau, staring at their tarnished little knobs, I remembered that at one time, long ago, I used to imagine that scene over and over again: as I burst into the bedroom with a rapier, as I furiously stick it into his broad back, high up, on the shoulders, covered in sparse bristles, low down smooth, as if inviting the blow. Now I felt neither fury nor disgust, nor the desire to murder, but just astonishment, weariness, and something like shame.

Like the time when Gumersinda told me that his last words had been: "Martín, my beloved, I'm coming..."

Jacek Dehnel

Mariano:

The day before yesterday the chambermaid woke Mama late in the evening; she ushered in Felipe, who had just arrived from the Quinta del Sordo; he insisted that the matter was extremely urgent and "the master will be very angry if I come back empty-handed"; my father had told him to fetch out all my grandfather's papers, "especially the most well-hidden ones, anything to be found at the bottom of the drawer, and letters in particular"; I was sent for too, luckily I wasn't asleep yet, for our music-making had been prolonged (some new scores had arrived, this time from Vienna, and Concepción and I had spent the entire evening trying a new sonata, and then we had sat down to whist and faro), so I went to my grandparents' house and spent a good two hours raking through cupboards, shelves and various drawers in search of everything that my father could have in mind; I went to bed in the middle of the night, exhausted and covered in dust. Only next morning – or rather I should say at noon – did I ask myself the question: why? Why all of a sudden, in a panic, displace documents from thirty or forty years ago? But at the time, in the middle of the night, I got enough of an answer from the look in Felipe's eyes, as he periodically repeated: "The master is waiting, the master will be very angry."

Perhaps as a man grows older he has to get used to the eccentricities of other people's old age; the easier it will then be to get used to the eccentricities of his own.

Javier:

That picture had to be here somewhere, and it was, brought

in with lots of others for Mariano's wedding, removed from Madrid purely by accident, for it would never have entered anyone's head to hang it in the rooms the wedding guests were going to pass through. I could remember him hiding it from me, so I wouldn't see what the little figures were up to, and I could remember that he painted it in two identical versions, something he almost never did – I'm not sure how much one was a true copy of the other, but I know they stood side by side on two easels, while he ranted that making copies was for silly young women, not for real painters. I also know that he sent one to Zapater, and kept the other to the end of his life hidden away, and even when I inherited all the paintings with the division of the estate and wrote descriptions of them, painting a little cross and a number on the back, he set this one aside from the pile, so that to this day it has never appeared in the inventory,

Now, as I dug it out of one of the wardrobes, along with other scenes that were inappropriate for a house hosting a wedding, and unwrapped it from thick brown canvas, I could examine it closely, but I still couldn't understand a thing. It was, apparently, a madhouse, perhaps the one in Zaragoza, where Uncle and Aunt Lucientes died; maybe while visiting them, as a young boy, he had feasted his eyes on these types, whom he painted many years later? Against an illuminated wall, in which a window appears high up, open to the white-hot sky, but barred, there is a crowd of half-naked men. This one is in a basinet with feathers and a wooden sword, being kissed on the hand by a hooded man in spectacles; that one, wearing a crown and a chain, surely plaited from straw pulled from their pallets, is blessing his subjects; closer to, in the middle, another one is sitting on the ground with his back to us: he is putting a bull's horns to his head, now one, now the other. Another man is kneeling, praying ardently, another is rolling about on the floor, writhing and screaming. A muscular man in a tricorne hat, aiming a non-existent gun, may have been a soldier, or maybe a hunter; right behind him another, hunched over, is riding a hobby horse. Against a pillar sits a man who may once have been a card sharp – he has stuck cards under the ribbon around his head, he is holding a candle or a sceptre and he is singing, singing with his eyes shut.

I couldn't understand any of it, I couldn't see any sign, or any clue, until, as I was wrapping the picture up again to put it away in the wardrobe, while holding it by the upper-right corner of the canvas, I saw that at the edge, deep in the shadows, there were two more figures, two men. One is standing with his legs set wide apart, tensed, leaning back, the other is kneeling in front of him, with the black stain of his head beneath a white patch of shirt – grey-brown in the gloom.

I knew those two lunatics, I had seen them before, drawn in the margins of the letters. Now the one whose lips were free was saying to the other: we are madmen.

XXXVI

Men Reading

Do not be misled by the respectable long beard and the sheared tonsure: if that is a monk, he serves in the black orders, and the page from which he is reading the words has been torn not from a missal, but from a book of spells and arcana.

No mass is ever heard with such zeal as those tar-coated words, prompting terror and disgust, but which are lapped up voraciously; those half-closed eyes, those lips quivering under the moustache, the ears throbbing with redness, the tremors running under the sweat-soaked cloth of the shirt. Here is the inner circle of those who have sealed a pact with their own blood and attained initiation into the mysteries – their broad backs hide the page and the symbols written on it from the common crowd.

Those who go on standing see only the consequence: the long curling horns growing from the skull of the magus in the white robe, a manifestation of power, a visible sign that lurking under the surface are forces and abominations to which few men have access.

Those who share in the power at once become weak, for the curved horns betray them from afar as knowing. But the painter comes to their help, who – even if he does not belong to the secret brotherhood – does not wish to reveal their secret. Quick as a flash, he paints over the great horns with white, then a shade of brown, and where they were growing straight out of the tumescent skull, he adds the head of a bearded man, raising his eyes to heaven in a mute prayer. Who will ever notice?

XXXVII

Javier:

I searched not just the entire bureau, but several other pieces of furniture too, a wardrobe in the old part of the house, and the attic. And I raked through everything – in the end it was here, not in the city, that he lived before his flight to Bordeaux. And yet I could not find the other half of this correspondence; I sent Felipe to Madrid, who came back at dawn with three baskets full of totally unneeded documents: old bills from people selling paints, canvases, brushes and glues, reminders from the royal chancellery, documents from the tapestry factory, invitations, refusals, confirmations, and a list of prices for plots of land. I even found a genealogical tree in there, which the old badger had ordered from some learned historian and which had proved disappointingly short. But not one little page of obscenities.

The nights of arduous toil over the paintings meant that as soon as something seized me, I might not go to bed at all, just keep working, until the hunger driving me on had been satisfied. Dawn was already breaking, when I decided to examine my father's bureau more carefully than before. I removed all the papers from it, all the keepsakes, old tin boxes full of sand for letters, corks from bottles, bits of string, utterly ground-down pens, and then onwards: the little drawers, the big drawers, everything, everything, until just the skeleton was left, eloquently revealing a secret drawer and the mechanism for opening it.

And that is where they were.

On top lay a small slip of paper folded several times, clearly thrown in later; I took it out and set it to one side; under it there was a fat wad of slightly decaying letters with ragged edges, tied with a piece of string, and at the very bottom a black bow.

I untied the string and began to read. I took a few pages from the top and sought their equivalents from the little pile of those other letters; they were like long rows of buttons and holes, like the corresponding grooves and teeth in the cog-wheels of a piece of machinery. I glanced at my watch – I still had a few hours; Zapater's nephew had agreed to pay me a visit at noon.

Only now did that life, my father's life, or at least the part of it to which we had no access, about which we had no idea, take on shapes and colours. Long waiting for rare encounters, for hunting trips together, roaming about the woods and bestial coupling in tents – they avoided inns and taverns, because they were afraid someone would find them in a situation which could not be explained to the judges at any tribunal and which would have plunged even the king's painter and a freshly ennobled businessman into tremendous trouble and infamy, if it didn't lead them straight to the stake.

My father's letters were bawdier, full of obscene jokes and caricatures, closer to the earth and to earthly matters: eating, money, things which had to be arranged for life to run smoothly; Zapater wrote tenderly like a young lady; I couldn't imagine the broad-shouldered man with the big nose – of whom I had a foggy memory from chance encounters and short stays in our house, many long years ago, and whom I now remembered in various representations from the vulgar drawings in the margins of the letters – being capable of choosing his words so tenderly, not to say sentimentally. How many tears there were, how much heart and how many sighs... and at the same time in almost every letter at least one little page was devoted to the most obscene descriptions of what men might do with each other, if they are utterly corrupted and sin against their own nature. If a man with a soul as cold as mine were to believe in Satan, then perhaps only after reading this sort of letter, where following the most affectionate expressions and delicate laments there appears a bit about *riding my rough arse hard* or *licking out your nest as you take my rod and its two bald companions all the way, as far as it can go down your throat.* I shifted my gaze to the other side of the desk top, where a week later, having read all this, my father had written back about some outstanding debt and the price of a pair of good mules in Madrid; I didn't know how to take it all in, I couldn't find the words or thoughts that would allow me to come to terms with this stream of manure and the unhealthy, nauseating sweetness that one ageing man had sent to another, in the name of some long-ago schoolboy groping which, through the weakness of their willpower, they had never been able to renounce.

And for all those years. So many years. Alongside twenty inseminations of his own wife and God only knows how many inseminations of other bellies, alongside countless affairs, frequenting brothels, having a go at models brought home from taverns, covering the holy pictures in the studio, there was that separate life, steeped in the most repulsive sin of all. He may have been deaf, but were we listening attentively enough?

I did not read everything; a letter full of sighs and affection, in the middle of which a large, clear shape appeared, with no writing, carefully drawn around with a pen, did its work; in any case, the young Zapater was due to arrive soon. I quickly gathered up the letters, tied them and threw them in the secret drawer, then set about putting all the drawers, large and small, back in the right places.

"The gentleman who came yesterday, to see you, sir," said Felipe, standing in the doorway. I replied that he was to take him into the garden and sit him on a stone bench under a tree. Let him wait – I'll be there in a moment.

"Well then?" asked the little man, when I came down into the garden, "did you find them?" After which he leaped towards me; he wasn't sitting on the bench, of course, he was walking, tripping, and jumping up and down, occasionally wrapping himself tighter in his mantle, for that day a cold wind was blowing from the direction of the city. I said I hadn't found anything, and he may do with my father's letters as he wished – after all, he had inherited them. They were of no use to me, and as for the nonsense contained in some of the notes, everyone knows that Francisco Goya suffered from a severe malady which had entirely deprived him of hearing, and partially of his wits as well, and that sometimes even in his letters he happened to write the most dreadful idiocies, which were dictated to him by passing fits of insanity.

I don't know what he wanted to say in reply, because he was so dumbfounded that I disappeared before he could manage to answer. I went into the room and tried hard to get back to work again, but I knew that until I had locked and covered the bureau, the whole mess would never let me paint. There now lay nothing on the unfolded desk top but the scraps which had been living in the secret drawer: the black bow and the blank, much folded slip of paper. I unfolded it – from inside fell a lock of dark hair with streaks of grey; the old fart's pitiful sentimentality; I wonder whether he took his fancy man a bow too as an eternal keepsake? No – in fact it was one of the duchess's bows from her black portrait!

Then I saw that on the slip of paper, in the middle, as on an open hand, where the curled lock lay, there were two short words, handwritten by my father: *La Pepa.*

Javier:

I threw myself onto the bed just as I was, in my clothing. And I got up in my clothing, I don't know how many hours later – in any case it was already dark – with the image before my eyes, just as once before, years ago, I had seen the Colossus, in minute detail. And without even rinsing my mouth, I walked at a steady pace into the room on the ground floor; I stood facing a foolish little scene showing a dancing peasant. I lit candles, brought up a ladder and mixed the paints. Each patch of white and each broad strip of black was placed in exactly the spots where I wanted it, covering the hills, the raised arms and legs, bits of sky and grass, the whole of that ridiculous blue-and-green idyll, in which man does not destroy, does not devour, does not rape, and does not smother, but leaps up and down with a smile on his crude face. I left myself the subtleties of penumbra for later; for now I used broad brushes to ladle the paint from two pails and threw on thick layers of brightness and darkness: the primordial gloom from which, extracted by a shaft of harsh light, a hungry body emerges.

XXXVIII

Saturn

Is there anything greater in the world than your appetite?
You've already eaten six and now you're devouring the
seventh; once in a while you interrupt your chewing (in the

never-ending darkness the echo of crunching arm bones goes on reverberating for ages, of finger joints rattling in the vast cavern beneath your palate, of blood and saliva pouring by the pailful over your flickering tongue); you spit, belch loudly and berate the headless body which you're squeezing so hard in your muscular great fingers that the knuckles are white, the child's skin is tearing and thick, bright blood is flowing from under it: "You oaf, you clod, you slob, you fatso," you say, "you layabout, you cringer, you parasite, you stinking idler, you impotent, you weakling, you weed, you amoeba," you say, "you mistake, you trash, you mooncalf, you ordure." You hawk and spit, and sink your teeth in once again, right up to the elbow, you rip out scraps of flesh, tendons, and shreds of skin. "See how fat you've grown – you look like a woman, look at that larded female rump of yours, like a wench's arse, and one of those fatter ones too, fight, kick! But you do nothing, you've let your legs dangle, you have no arms, you have no head, how will you stuff yourself now, you hog? Be a man! Be a man!"

And trembling all over, slavering, you shake me, until I bump my feet against your great, erect prick. The more you devour, the stiffer it stands, against the entire world, against all the darkness, which you will smother and possess, and ride on, and devour. You screw everything and everyone, without exception, your semen is like drops of acid for etching copper plates, wherever it falls, it bites in deep; then you'll knock off a couple more portraits, you'll buy a piece of land, you'll gobble up a four-course dinner, hunt down a few partridges and a hare, engrave a very elegant *Capricho*, hammer a chambermaid, and straight after her a dark beauty from the inn who's posed for you as the Blessed Virgin – just a moment, you'll just cover the little picture of Our Lady of Zaragoza with a cloth, then along the way you'll drink a cup of chocolate on the hoof and sketch the head of a guinea fowl for a still life – and you're back already, you're riding the dark girl, you bite off my other arm, send a few *billets doux* to a certain tradesman, tear yourself away from your saturnine studio just briefly to inseminate your wife, and then, after dark you'll still finish off a large, heroic allegory, while whistling a *zarzuela* and sticking candle after candle to the brim of your hat, as fast as they burn down.

For everything around you burns down, elapses, is effaced, or grows old, and you alone, staring ever more goggle-eyed, keep feasting on whatever comes to hand; still strong and muscular, even if rounded here and there, even if your long, dirty locks and tousled beard have had time to go grey; when there's nothing in the vicinity you devour your children, that's why you keep on living, virtually without end; and even when you finally fall and vomit up not six children, but just one, it turns out it was in your stomach for a bit too long to be master of the thunderbolts and the peak of Olympus. You spit out a little old man with a double chin, who wakes up in slime and bile, well chewed, but made whole again; he feels his arms and belly uncertainly and walks away, stupefied. As if he had no destiny.

XXXIX

Javier:

I painted for two hours perhaps, maybe four, maybe five
– it was still night, and through the windows on both sides
of Saturn I could see just the same darkness as the gloom
stretching away behind him; beyond there was his Malady
with knife in hand, and the black He-goat casting a spell on
the young postulant, and further scenes, separated from each
other by the black windows and the darkness filling the open
door; I walked around the stacks of furniture, along the walls,
holding a candelabra, and examined each of the paintings,
the successive parts of the great darkness that engulfs the
world, men, women, children and demons, in which we build
our nests, through which we battle our way like moles and
larvae underground – as far as the eye can reach, blackness,
blackness and more blackness. In the main room, in the hall,
on the stairs. What in the daytime had colours, was now
evenly black, though in various shades: bluish where the light
of a thin, sharpened moon was falling through the windows,
brownish where the warm glow of the candles extended. Above
the black steps of the splendid staircase – a black balustrade,
higher up, black canvases in black frames, worth a great many
black doubloons and even more black *reales* and *maravedís*.
And, against the high window looking into blackness, a great
black head on a black pedestal, round as a cannon ball, hard

as a bull's poll, with a vast brow that repels every blow, that butts its way through life, pushing everything and everyone aside, with even deeper, even more pitch-dark blackness under the overhang of the thick eyebrow arches, the eyes completely blank, fixed only on himself, turned to the inside.

That he needs, that he always needed: to look around him. He was not just deaf, but also blind, so it was time someone finally opened his eyes for him. I set down the candelabra. Fortunately Mariano had economized, and instead of paying a sculptor, he had only had the plaster painted to look like proper marble, thanks to which the head is lighter, and even a rather portly fifty-year-old can lift it from its pedestal.

I grabbed hold of it firmly, moved it from the pedestal, and as it slid off, shifting its entire weight onto my hands, I could hardly stay upright – but I told myself I could manage – after all, I was used to it, I had carried this burden for decades, so I could bear it for a little longer.

First I carried it downstairs – a pity I couldn't hold both head and candles at once; I was moving very slowly, carefully testing with a foot to be sure I didn't step on an abandoned bowl or stick, or bump my hip against a chair or a doorknob, because I didn't want to smash the head, I merely wanted to show it the *whole* work. Now that it was completed. I knew those pictures by heart, and it was looking with eyes which didn't need the light to see anything; and so we were moving about in total darkness and silence, not counting the scraping of branches against the roof tiles in the other wing of the house.

We walked around the entire main room on the ground floor, we saw Evil whispering in an ear, and empty-headed people who only believe someone with a famous name, a *cocotte* changed into a woman in mourning, and a black he-goat seducing a very young girl with a muff, we saw Malady, and the insatiable Saturn. We stood in front of him the longest, so long that I had to set down my burden on top of a chest of drawers (shortly before I had banged my elbow so hard against its protruding edge that a shock had run up my arm, almost making me drop the head). I was out of breath. "What a foolish old fart you are," I said to myself, "have you got a screw loose, eh, Javier? Everyone'll think you've gone completely mad." But I hadn't spent thirty years asleep, if not longer, just to be concerned about what people would say now, or rather what they would have said if they had seen me here, the father of a family, a respected citizen, lugging a piece of plaster about the house in the middle of the night, wearing a paint-soiled shirt. Plaster pretending to be marble. And what's more, talking to this plaster pretending to be marble.

It was hardest of all on the stairs; with each step it was heavier going. And yet we did it, we managed to clamber upstairs.

By now the sky was a bit lighter. Not light, but lighter, and between the procession of the Inquisition and the scarlet cape of the goddess fluttering above the battle field, I could see the dawn rising over livid-blue Madrid, illuminating the wall opposite; I set the head on the first chair to hand, sat myself down next to it and looked, we both looked, at those two men floundering up to their knees in thick mud, as they laid about each other with cudgels.

Only now did I notice how similar they were. The same thick eyebrows and sideburns, the same short-tailed jackets hugging their broad shoulders; they were the mirror image of each other, locked in combat – equal in height, they only differed in one way, by age. But in time the one who was younger would come to resemble the older man. He would speak in his words and come to know his secrets, and in his head, when he fell asleep, exactly the same phantoms would appear.

We did not examine the rest of the pictures; I took hold of the head with a firm grip and carried it down to the landing between the floors, where it had its place.

Mariano:

In the autumn Fatso's health improved; he abandoned his incessant painting and repainting of the walls, and allowed Felipe to put away all the pails, buckets, palettes and brushes, while he took care of supervising the strong men who put the furniture back in its right place, and then the washerwomen, whom he agreed to have clean the main rooms on the ground floor and upstairs, so that – not counting the repugnant scenes which continue to menace on the walls and which he will not permit to be painted over or even covered up – the house has started to look normal again. Although Concepción still refuses to make trips there in the summer, as we used to, not even one-day outings with baskets of food and instruments, for an afternoon meal by the river and some music-making in the evening.

Not that he was entirely well – in any case, has he ever been well? But with the passage of time I must take more care of my own family and of myself, and not my father, who has my mother to help him, the servants, and all too many silver *reales* – and those *reales* can do things not even my mother or the servants can manage.

For a young man from a good family, pretty good times have set in; they say the queen wants to strike out at the Carlists, by confiscating and selling off church lands – there's nothing for it but to invest. One also hears about mines from Roman times, where apparently there are immense deposits of various metals, and information about them, so they say, can be bought at a very affordable price. Well, and of course there are the railways.

The de Goya family tree, which Fatso found in my grandfather's archive, requires some serious addenda, but I'm already aware that now the grandees have been restored to the kingdom, we will have to embellish our coat-of-arms with a title. And quickly too, for they'll grow dearer in a trice.

Javier:

I do not feel as if I have outlived that great, deaf old bull: the mass of muscles under folds of fat and sagging skin, the mighty skeleton of a giant and the reminiscences of successive triumphs and conquests, which burned in that old stove to the end: real hunting trips with kings and invented fights in the arena, models screwed in the corner behind the stretchers, on the go, between one brush stroke and the next, for the paint had to dry out a bit, and La Alba, on whom he never laid a finger, but through murmurs and smirks he tried to give the impression that he had been the greatest love of her life; it was from there, from those truths and delusions, that the juices flowed, which both fertilized and purged him for so many years; it was thanks to them that he wriggled out of illness after illness: yellow fever, bad blood, paralysis. And black bile abides in me, carving out its corridors like a weevil in soft wood.

I spend whole days in peace and quiet now; every few months some customer for my father's pictures appears: a Frenchman, an Englishman, or a German. Merchant, lord or painter, it's all the same to me – ever since they've been writing in the guide books to Spain that at my house one can buy something left behind by the great Goya I cannot complain of a lack of prospective buyers. But what a fuss it involves! I never let anyone in off the street; one must make an appointment in advance, for an hour; the maid knows that if anyone insists and says he is just about to leave Madrid, that in a moment, any second now, he has a post coach, even so she is to refuse; one way or another he will come the next day. I receive them in the library, never in the studio – some people, especially the painters, insist that they would like to see "the workroom". Out of the question. I show them albums full of drawings – different every time, for now and then I amuse myself by rearranging the pages, changing the order, taking some apart and combining them into others. I show them paintings, by the old man, and by others. They smack their lips and express their admiration, and then the bargaining begins. "Not for sale," I say. "Not for sale. This one's not for sale either. Nor is this one." Finally, stupefied, they take a drawing which I knocked off a week earlier out of boredom, and they pay a fortune for it, convinced they've made an excellent deal.

For of course I still draw sometimes. A little in pencil, a little in pen and ink. I do not paint. I haven't the strength for it, or even the need – everything I was to paint, I painted long ago, on those walls, which now I never see at all. The house stands empty, and I like to imagine how in winter water seeps through the flimsy walls made of cheap, sun-baked bricks, how the mildew effloresces on the witches' faces, how the black lines of cracks, night after night, for they are nocturnal travellers, laboriously toil their way from one end of a picture to the other, how pieces of plaster fall off the walls and lie on the floor, behind the chest of drawers, behind the sofa. Someone's finger, a wisp of brown cloud. Felipe died long ago, Mariano never actually went there when the children were little, or after the death of Marianito, my cunning favourite, who wormed his way out in time, nor once María had grown up; Concepción says that it's impossible to live there, that it's like eating in a morgue, like playing the violin in a slaughterhouse. She thinks that when she plays the violin, or when she eats anywhere at all, in the entire world, she is not eating in a morgue, and not playing in a slaughterhouse.

But even if I don't paint, I still think up pictures and their titles. A donkey in a tail coat (I can see exactly his dark ears and his smug, vacant little eyes), scattering mouldy grain for some moulting cockerels: it is Mariano, trying to catch a withered old grandee in order to buy a title from him for the rest of his estate; but the cockerels aren't stupid, and before one of them finally agrees to sell his red comb, they'll all have had time to eat their fill and to waddle off to another donkey. For there is no shortage of donkeys. *There's No Shortage of Donkeys*, that's a good title, but not quite good enough. *There's Never a Lack of These*? No, it'll look as if there's never a lack of cockerels. Which is also true. *There's Never a Lack of These or Those*. Too long. Or this: *They Won't Forgive* – two chopped-off heads on pikes, one sinking its teeth into the other one. I saw that throughout my youth. A cheery old man, sucking the marrow from some tiny bones, while a succession of children crowds in the doorway. *Suffer the Little Children to Come Unto Me*. Good, eh?

Sometimes I am amazed by the precision with which I see each of these pictures – a little like then, long ago, when *The Colossus* appeared to me in minute detail, but in a different way. Then I had an overall vision, now I can see each brush stroke; I can see the exact shade of the paint and I know how to obtain it, I choose the thickness of the brush – sometimes I dream of my favourite brushes, with which I painted at the Quinta, one in particular, almost completely eaten away, for the plaster quickly uses up the hairs, coated at the very tip with a crust of hardened black – I know how to guide my hand while applying the white to an old man's sweating brow, how to pick out the vermilion-pinkish blush, not youthful, but in fact senile; the backrest of the chair on which that glutton for bones is sitting: every glint, every shadow, I can see it all, everything. And that is quite enough for me. My son, my son-in-law and my granddaughter are sure I waste the day away on nothing, that my head is full of festering, stagnant waters with nothing going on in them, but they have no idea what is born in a head from year after year of inactivity, out of decaying residues; they have no idea about the growing strength, which keeps pressing on the sluices and dams, and which might break them down at any moment, flooding the entire vicinity, and splashing the walls with the most monstrous images.

XL

Javier:

It's a wonder that only now have rumours reached me that Rosario Weiss, that last hope of my father's that his loins would produce a great artist, that little chickabiddy devoid of any talent, who first of all dabbled away at miniatures, then wallpaper, and then copies of the old masters, did in fact manage to achieve something. She made such a fine fake of some little canvas that a wicked, wicked, naughty dealer sold it as an original. There was a bit of a stink about it, and the Duchess de San Fernando had even forbidden her to copy Velázquezs, for they were "too much alike".

All this was brought to me by Gumersinda, of course, who in her inimitable way knows every bit of gossip in Madrid before anyone else hears about it – and every time she came to me, covered in blushes, saying: "You'll never guess what's up with that wretched little girlie who tried to snatch our property!" – and I just agreed, for I was hardly going to argue with her that it wasn't the girlie who tried to rob us, but we who tried to rob her, or rather her mother, and we didn't just try, we did take away her property, blatantly lying over my fast-fading father as he lay stretched out on his death bed.

Either way, Rosario finally did quite well out of her painting, for she was given the position of drawing mistress to a fat, ugly little girl who just happens to be the Infanta of

Spain. But suddenly, half a year later she emerged from the palace and ran straight into a street riot, and was so distressed by it that she came down with a terrible infection and died. Since then Gumersinda has never spoken of her otherwise than as "that poor little girlie"; in any case she has rarely spoken of her at all, for corpses are not often the subject of gossip worth repeating.

But if – I thought to myself – after the miniatures and the wallpaper, the copies and the dabbling, anyone still had any doubts that a great talent had been living here among us, and it was just that fate had been unfavourable to it, then at this point he'd have to capitulate; anybody who suffers a terrible infection and gets the vapours at the sight of a screaming crowd should stick to accessories: wallpaper, teaching infantas and painting scenes on fans. A real artist does not need smelling salts.

And then I remembered her mother: nipped in at the waist, robust, laughing a lot and loud, dragging my father to circuses and to entertainments; how she would watch animal fights, how voraciously she consumed mountains of food, and I thought: was that small girl, was little Ladybird, as I was, eaten away day by day, devoured, torn to pieces? Was the bed in Bordeaux the bed of two predators, carnivores, child-eaters, who were just made for each other, who sniffed each other out with their animal sense of smell and said to one another: "I know your horrible secret"?

Mariano:

My father lives like a pig in clover from selling the pictures left by my grandfather, and yet I am well aware that he very carefully estimates what he can sell, and what is still worth keeping in the studio, on the walls of the Madrid house, and at the Quinta del Sordo; he has a complete catalogue of prints, drawings and paintings in his head, and he is able to price them in seconds flat, to give the year and the place of production, and sometimes to come up with an amusing anecdote about a chicken which the cook swiped from a still life and tossed in the pot, or about an impatient model.

I have my suspicions – I know for example that he still sends the chambermaid's son to Ezquerra's shop, where in his day my grandfather used to buy brushes, paints and glues, and that Ezquerra still supplies him with package after package of goods, which disappear behind the studio door, as if nothing were up.

About two months ago I took myself off to Manzanares to show Manuel, who plays trios with us, the old piano standing in the House of the Deaf Man; I hadn't been there for at least two years, if not four, and even if Felipe's idiot son looks after the house, time is doing its work; the roof has lost some tiles, the plaster is covered in big stains, like the map of an alien world, the paint is peeling from the doors and windows, and the shoots of creepers are slowly, but diligently crumbling the walls. In the old part, which I only dropped into for a moment, the building could collapse entirely, there are so many cracks in the walls and so many rotten beams in the ceiling; the great staircase still looks monumental, but with no one living in it, the entire house is decomposing from the inside; in an imperceptible way it is changing into fine dust, turning into felt; the furniture has grown ugly, the wallpaper had become unfashionable, the piano has gone out of tune and a decision is needed whether to call out the tuner there, or transport the instrument to the city and restore it to a usable state once it is at our house; for lately Concepción has taken a fancy to the idea of concerts for two pianos, and as she has been feeling a little worse lately, I would like to give her a small pleasure. Only my father's scrawls were just as hideous as ever. Poor Manuel, whose father was a wheelwright and who wants at any cost to pass for a connoisseur and an educated man, was just as delighted by my grandfather's masterpieces, hanging on the staircase, as by the daubs in the music room; I didn't let my surprise show, but later, back at home, Concepción and I laughed heartily about it.

Only that night, as I lay in bed listening to her restless, heavy breathing, tossing and turning, did I suddenly think of a particular transaction that might actually bring me a decent profit.

Javier:

Now the twilight is coming on, and it is time to own up. To everything. Yes, it's true, my name, surname and address could be found in the English guidebooks to Spain, and yes, it said there that I was willing to show the old man's works from "a unique private collection". It also said that it may be possible, "after a little bargaining", to persuade me to sell this and that; this reference cost me two small drawings, which are either still hanging at the home of that arrogant English, puffed-up pen-pusher, or have long since made their way, for a nice round sum in guineas, into the collection of some equally smug and equally bloated lord with gout.

Yes, it's true, I loved having those visitors, that sort of visitor; sometimes they were so dull-witted that they would come into my study, announced by the maid, with the guidebook still in their hands, and a finger on page 158, where it was suggested that from the naive Javier Goya one could buy a masterpiece for very little money. Yes, it's true, I elaborated this technique right down to the last detail and it always worked – they were so similar to one another that it couldn't fail to work. They always treated me with a mixture of feigned respect and forbearing, such as swindlers have towards persons whom they are shortly intending to hoodwink. They would assure me they had come to Madrid purely in order to see the works of "the great Goya" (few of them spoke in our language, they were almost always accompanied by an interpreter, so I had to hear about "the great Goya" once in English, and a second time in Spanish, ad nauseam, every compliment, every bit of flattery twice over), and I would simper, saying this was just the remains of the collection, that I had sold almost everything, and that the most valuable items had been bought by "grand gentlemen, including many Englishmen", if the visitor happened to be an Englishman. Because there were also Frenchmen who came, and even two Germans. They'd wheedle and cajole – after all, they hadn't come just to be sent away empty-handed, so finally, always performing the same heavy sigh, I would show them into the studio. The maid wasn't allowed to clean it on pain of dismissal – I cultivated the dust in there, the chaos, the mugs full of brushes with crusted paint on their forked, splayed hairs, thanks to which they felt as if they were entering a long-forgotten sanctuary of art. They looked, but now there wasn't any more admiration in their gaze, there was nothing but rapacity; I could see their irises changing into big round coins. And that is why I had no scruples.

Yes, it's true that it was I who painted most of the pictures by that old stuffed shirt, Francisco Goya y Lucientes, which now adorn lordly residences, and before which connoisseurs and experts smack their lips. Yes, it's true it was I who drew those drawings, it was I who spent evenings in a little room behind the wardrobe, where on bits of old paper black-haired *majas* came into being, witches, imprisoned convicts, and lunatics. It was I, without making any mess at all, without splashing paint to left and right, without becoming at all conceited, and without sticking candles all around my hat, but quite calmly and steadily, at my natural pace, who produced valuable souvenirs from Madrid for those sly fellows with the guidebook in their hands, marking page 158 with a finger. I spread dust-coated portfolios in front of them, I wrestled with a small drawer ("I haven't opened it for five years!" – that was my *pièce de résistance*), and then I would groan, whimper and complain of dire poverty, and offer them a price which might seem a little steep, but even so was just a small fraction of the favours that would rain down on them once they had hung the framed painting or drawing in a place of honour in the parlour, and they would be proudly saying: "This inconspicuous slip of paper, this little canvas is a real dowry for my daughter. A Goya. A genuine Goya, not so well known here yet, but on the continent he's a very famous name. I bought it from his hare-brained son for a pittance."

As I bid them farewell – this I was never able to deny myself – I would toss in: "And do you know, sir, I am a painter too", and keeping the same friendly, doltish look on my face, I would watch them squirm and get tangled in their answers: "Oh, that's splendid! What a pity I have to go now!", "I'm sure they're no match for your father's works! Alas, my carriage awaits!" or "My son is a merchant too!" One of them said with that terrible accent of his: "You're a chip off the old block." "Here," I replied, nodding, "we say that the apple doesn't fall far from the apple tree. Ah, these old adages!"

I don't know why I didn't want to talk about this earlier. I just didn't want to, that's all; a man grows stubborn in his old age. It seemed to me that only one work should remain after me, the one which no Englishman in a travelling cape, with calculating eyes set in a waxen face, would ever have bought: the scrawls of a senile old man, whole yards of wasted rosebud-patterned calico, plastered over, covered in ugliness and abomination, the walls of a respectable house (and when was it ever respectable? Before the old man bought it perhaps) changed into alehouse daubs. It seemed to me shameful to be adding my nice little accessories to that, the items from my one-man miniature factory, where I produced witches and *majas*, demons and dead guinea fowl, drawings, small paintings and prints, my own illicit little range, my conjuring tricks for foreign visitors. Highly profitable too. What on earth could have given me the impression that I was able to paint as well as he, when I had already shown I was able to paint better long before?

Those were just an old fogey's amusements. The money didn't matter, but that moment when I would tell them, right on the doorstep, that in fact, I too... oh! The worst botches, which I would have been ashamed to sell – though there would certainly have been willing buyers – didn't end up in the oven; I wrapped them in paper, tied it with string and shoved them under the chest of drawers. After my death that idiot, who will inherit everything from me, will sell them on a par with his grandfather's greatest masterpieces, I am totally convinced of that. And that will be my final victory, from beyond the grave; in fact, what I painted at the House of the Deaf Man will disintegrate and disappear irretrievably, for it is already peeling in flakes of paint and falling to the floor with crumbs of plaster, in fact no one will remember me otherwise than as "old Goya's indolent son", of whom no one will really know what he did, but my fool of a son will take in a couple more fools, and they'll hang my worst botches in their sumptuous residences – bah, maybe they'll even send them to the royal collections. And other fools will stand in front of them. And smack their lips. And go into raptures. And smack their lips. And go into raptures again.

Well, I must say, that amuses me.

XLI

Mariano:

So I am the last – neither my grandfather, nor my father, nor little Mariano Javier is alive. The doctors do not give Concepción more than a year and a half. Unless I were to have another try, unless I were to be the doting bridegroom again. But what for? Well, anything is still possible, I feel young and full of strength.

After the old man's death I started to put things in order; I exported everything of any value at all from the Quinta del Sordo: paintings, the more precious furniture, my grandfather's archive. I spent two months sorting out the papers: drawings, prints, letters and documents. In a secret drawer in the bureau I found a whole wad of vulgar, filthy little letters and some bits of rubbish; all this – out of concern for the memory of the great Goya – I burned. I made a rough estimate of the value of what I had inherited, and decided to put my clever plan into action.

I knew that in Bordeaux my grandfather had been closest to Brugada; but for years Brugada had been unable to come from France, because he would at once have ended up in prison for his views; whenever he had some ongoing estate or property affairs, he invariably sent a representative – the chances of him coming to Madrid and catching me red-handed were thus negligible. Not to say non-existent.

Therefore I went into the studio and took out several large

sheets of the old paper on which my grandfather used to sketch, and then I sat down at a small table and started to write out an inventory for the House of the Deaf Man. Room by room, item by item.

A mahogany bed with a double headrest, transformed by day into a sofa for sitting on, a fire screen, two firedogs, bellows and tongs, *idem* a bureau, side tables, corner tables with marble tops, *idem* an old armchair covered in cordwain, viols, a piano, *idem* twelve chairs upholstered in green, twelve cherry-wood chairs from Vitoria, an English mahogany side table with music stands, donated by don Mariano de Goicoechea... I felt as if I were there once again, walking about among the furniture, stopping, picking up some trinket from the chest of drawers, and putting it back in its place... and also paintings by the great Goya. This portrait, another portrait, *idem* a still life with a turkey, a portrait of the Duchess of Alba in widow's attire, in a mantilla, *idem* a painting depicting a colossus against a battle field, fourteen pictures decorating the walls, painted directly onto the walls of the music room upstairs and the drawing room downstairs, *idem* a small table for handicrafts... as if it were all quite normal. And I started to look for a buyer for the house, in which just before departing for France the great Goya had painted masterpieces worth a fortune on the walls, worth more than the house itself made of sun-baked brick, in which perhaps only the monumental staircase might be of any use.

I did not even make any special effort; I wrote from memory – if there are any mistakes, so be it; Brugada was meant to have written it at my grandfather's bidding, and he, after all, never could remember what stood where, so he was ideally suited to the task of producing an inventory.

XLII

Mariano:

The day before yesterday I walked about the house – perhaps for the very last time. I clambered upstairs – ugh, in my fifty-third year of life it should cause me less difficulty; when my grandfather moved here he was more than twenty years older than I am now, and he wasn't so out of breath on the stairs, he never stopped half way up on the landing. I had to. I stood there, and rested against the slightly flaking plaster column, on which his fantastic, huge head used to stand until recently. The head of a genius. Ha, that was quite a head! In any case, I ordered it from a very good sculptor, I can't remember the name, money came to me easily in those days. And left me easily too. I suggested to del Colmenares that I could leave it here – after all, it is a memento, my grandfather's house, a special place. But perhaps I was demanding too much – maybe he'd have swallowed the hook if I had remembered that name? Never mind about that; I am leaving him the column, may he choke on it, and as for the head, which has been put away for now in a box full of wood shavings, some place will yet be found for it.

My father's blotches are falling apart, peeling off and coming unstuck everywhere. On the ground floor the damp rises from the ground every winter, even up there, on the hill; the ones upstairs are simply crumbling and disintegrating. It's enough to thump your hand – like this, thump, thump – and bits of plaster and paint come showering onto the ground. I don't know who will get those daubs in the end, and if he'll be indulgent towards them, because Colmenares is not likely to keep the house for himself, but to sell it on, fleecing me and the next purchaser like a profiteer, but someone is sure to take care of the matter. Either he'll call in some dauber to patch up the surface, or he'll have them hacked off and be done with it. Although, if Colmenares finds a customer for the house, it won't be thanks to the shrivelled remains of the vineyard (I inspected it for a few minutes from the window; and to think there was once a flourishing garden there!), the mouldering curtains and walls of dried brick; it's more likely to be that, yes, that's what will interest him, those scrawls.

I trailed downstairs and, in the lower left-hand corner of that picture of the horrible old man eating the child, I saw one more signature, overlooked when I was getting rid of the rest – I don't know how I could have failed to notice it. From a small pocket in my waistcoat I took out my old penknife, a present from my grandfather, with almost all its gilding worn away by now, and at a single stroke I chipped off the scrap inscribed: *Javier Goya y Bayeu, pintor*; just in case, I crushed it with my heel so that nothing could be deciphered, and I left. Colmenares was already climbing the hill in his unbuttoned frock coat; on seeing me he raised a hand to his top hat.

Ledig House, Omi, New York, 12 IX 2009 – Warsaw, 17 VIII 2010

From the author

Saturn would never have come about if not for the work of Professor Juan José Junquera who, while writing a book about Francisco Goya's *Black Paintings* commissioned by the Museo del Prado (*The Black Paintings of Goya*, Scala Publishers, 2003), was the first person to notice that the famous series of frescoes was most probably painted by someone else. Early references to these works are doubtful: one mentions some "caprices and caricatures of people who visited him" (which were probably destroyed while the Quinta del Sordo was being rebuilt), while a second, Brugada's famous inventory, apparently written by Goya's friend from Bordeaux is – as Junquera has pointed out – a fake, for it includes words which did not exist in the Spanish language at the time, and was most certainly drawn up in the 1860s or 1870s, presumably by Mariano Goya, as a way of selling the crumbling villa at a greater profit. Junquera has also pointed out that the part of the house in which the frescoes were painted was most probably built in 1830, after Francisco Goya's death, on the occasion of Mariano's wedding, while the presumed author of the monumental series of frescoes was none other than the artist's mysterious son, Javier, of whom we know almost nothing.

Junquera's theses were received with some incredulity, not to say anger. In January 2009 the Prado did however admit that another of Goya's canonical works, *The Colossus*, was painted by someone else, perhaps by Asensio Julià or another of the artist's imitators. Therefore we cannot exclude the possibility that one day there may yet be a change in the attribution of the *Black Paintings* as well.

The conjectural long-term homosexual affair between Goya and Zapater was first considered by Natacha Seseña in her work, *Goya y Las Mujeres* ("Goya and the Women", Satillana USA, 2005), but it is plainly in evidence from reading the artist's letters, edited by Sarah Symmons and translated by Philip Troutman (*Goya. A Life in Letters*, Pimlico, 2004). I also made extensive use of the biographies of Goya by Evan S. Connell (*Francisco Goya: A Life*, Counterpoint, 2004) and Robert Hughes (*Goya*, Vintage 2004), and of Julia Blackburn's charming book, *Old Man Goya* (Jonathan Cape, 2002), which describes the artist's last years, as well as the excellent catalogue from the exhibition *Goya's Last Works* held at the Frick Collection in New York in 2006.

Observant readers might occasionally notice divergences between what they are reading in the ekphrases of each of the paintings and what they are seeing in the reproductions. This is the result of the partial re-painting and alterations to which the *Black Paintings* were subjected – some of these changes (as for example the painting-out of Saturn's enormous erection, or the trimming of a broad strip of blank space behind the "postulant" in the "Witches' Sabbath", still visible in early photographs by Juan Laurent, showing the frescoes on the walls of the house) are certainly the work of Salvador Martínez-Cubells, who transferred onto canvas, renovated and at the same time altered all the frescoes from the House of the Deaf Man. Other sections (such as the horns above the "Men Reading" or the mourning version of "Leocadia") may have been re-painted by the original artist. He too definitely produced some banal rustic scenes of dancing peasants which disappeared under the layer of shocking images known to us today as the *Black Paintings*.

Finally I would like to express my gratitude to the staff of Ledig House at the Omi Arts Center in New York, thanks to whose kindness I was able to spend a month writing almost half of *Saturn* in conditions every writer should be able to enjoy.

Jacek Dehnel

The quotation on page 9 is from *Pascal Quignard le solitaire: Rencontre avec Chantal Lapeyre-Desmaison*, by Pascal Quignard and Chantal Lapeyre-Desmaisons, Les Fleurie Éditions, Paris, 201, p. 54:

Quand le présent offre peu de joie et que les mois qui sont sur le point de venir ne laissent présager que des répetitions, on trompe la monotonie par des assaults de passé. On pioche dans ce qu'on ne peut dire de sa vie à personne et on transporte ces petits poutres de bois et ces petits duvets des oiseaux dans un nid de vieille patricienne ou d'antiques Hébreux.

A small glossary of the less familiar Spanish words used in the text

afrancesados – "Francophiles" or "Frenchified", was the term used for Spaniards who were supporters of the French occupation of the Iberian peninsula, and of Enlightenment ideas and Liberalism in general.

almud – a measure of liquid equivalent to 4.625 litres.

birlocho – a kind of light, open carriage, a gig.

coroza – a pointed cap, which along with a sackcloth tunic called a *sambenito* (from San Benito because it had a shape reminiscent of a Benedictine monk's tunic) was the costume worn by those under trial or convicted by the Inquisition. The sinner's crime was written on it, along with relevant symbols: for those sentenced to death by burning, hell fire and devils (this costume was called the *samarra*), for those who saved their own lives by renouncing their evil deeds, turned-back flames (*fuego revolto*), as a sign that they had escaped death at the stake; and for common sinners, a Saint Andrew's cross (the actual *sambenito*, which in time came to signify all forms of penitential tunic).

fanega – a measure of ground equivalent to 0.643 hectares.

josefino – a supporter of Joseph I, in other words Joseph

Bonaparte, placed on the Spanish throne by Napoleon.

maja, majo – fashionable types who came from the common populace (especially in Madrid), and who wore rather exaggerated, colourful costumes (the last vestiges of which still remain in modern *toreador* costumes). *Majísmo* was a whole sub-culture with its own customs, entertainments and moral code, and also with a dislike of the *afrancesados* and *petimetres*, who favoured French customs.

marran – a Jew who has converted to Catholicism (often under coercion); these people were generally suspected of covertly practising Judaism and were persecuted by the Spanish Inquisition for almost its entire existence.

reales, maravedís, escudos – Spanish coins. In Goya's day there were 85 *maravedís* in one silver *real de plata fuerte*, or 2.5 *reales de vellón* (an alloy of copper and silver). There were 16 silver *reales* in one gold *escudo*.

sainete – a kind of short farce or comic sketch (usually from the life of the common populace), accompanied by music.

saturnismo – plumbism or lead poisoning.

seguidilla – a fast folk tune (sung and danced) originally from Castile, but now present in other regions of Spain.

zarzuela – a form of musical play that alternates between spoken and sung scenes, which include operatic and popular songs, as well as dance.

Main historical events

1746 Franciso Goya was born in Fuendetodos, Aragón.

1765 Goya went to Madrid and studied under court painter Anton Raphael Mengs.

1773 Goya married Josefa Bayeu (La Pepa), whose brother Francisco was one of his teachers.

1784 Javier Goya was born.

1799 Goya was appointed First Court Painter to King Charles IV. Goya's patrons included Prime Minister Manuel Godoy.

1808 French forces invaded Spain, leading to the Peninsular War of 1808–14.
The invasion was initially welcomed by Spaniards with Enlightenment views.
A coup d'état instigated by Napoleon ousted Charles IV from the Spanish throne, replacing him with his son Ferdinand, but then Napoleon installed his brother, Joseph, as king of Spain (popularly nicknamed *Pepe Botella*, "Joe Bottle").
On 2 May the citizens of Madrid rebelled against the French occupation and on 3 May the French carried out

mass executions in retaliation, famously recorded by Goya.

All the Spanish provinces rose against the French, who were forced to abandon Madrid and retreat across the River Ebro. In August the British landed an army in Portugal under the Duke of Wellington and allied with Spain and Portugal in the fight against the French.

1813 At the Battle of Vitoria the allied armies routed Joseph Bonaparte's army.

1814 The Spanish King Ferdinand VII was restored to the throne, popularly known as *El Deseado*, "the Desired One". Ferdinand nullified the Constitution and restored absolute monarchy, thus provoking the Carlist Wars.

1819 Goya bought the Quinta del Sordo just outside Madrid on the Manzanares River.

1824 Goya left Spain to live in Bordeaux.

1828 Goya died of a stroke in Bordeaux.